The Ginger Bottle

Marie Rowan

Published in 2019 by
Moira Brown
Broughty Ferry
Dundee. DD5 2HZ
www.publishkindlebooks4u.co.uk

Copyright © Marie Rowan

The right of Marie Rowan to be identified as the Author of this work has been asserted in accordance with the Copyrights, Designs and Patents Act 1988.

All rights reserved. No part of this book may be reprinted or reproduced or utilised in any form or by any electronic, mechanical or other means, now known or hereafter invented, including photocopying or recording, or any information storage or retrieval system, without the permission in writing from the Publisher.

ISBN: 978-1-0908-5122-2

Dedication:

This book is dedicated to Alan and Jean Goodall of New Zealand with much love.

Acknowledgement:

I should like to thank my good friend Charlie Garnett most sincerely for giving me permission to use his wonderful photograph as the cover for this book.

Chapter 1

The cold, brown, clawing fog hung about Loney's tall, lean frame like a sodden overcoat, seeping into his very bones, it seemed, and plastering his fair curly hair, such as there was of it, to his skull. Payment in kind. Loney had once squared Abbad the Barber's £45.55 newspaper account and Abbad had supplied the equivalent amount in haircuts. Loney knew he was being short-changed but there was now only one haircut left to go and then the worst barber ever to come out of Turkey would be in the clear. He heaved himself off the wall that secured – some hope! – the ground of the Old Calton Burial Ground and knew his dicky knee rendered him incapable of climbing over it right then. Everybody knew he had refused a knee replacement operation but none that it really had been a hip one. Loney had his pride. He was thirty-two and already felt relegated to life's sub's bench. But such embittered thoughts were not worthy of him, he decided. He sought once more the reassuring comfort of the three metres high wall and glanced at his watch. An anonymous figure loomed suddenly out of the fog, an envelope changed hands and Loney was glad he had remained at his post. A note the previous evening had been left for him in The Ginger Bottle suggesting that something to his advantage would be slipped to him outside the graveyard at that hour the following day. Traffic began to move again and the heavy silence of the previous few minutes was shattered as the lights changed and Abercromby Street became, once more, a concrete river as this busy Glasgow thoroughfare sluiced its users at speed on their way to and from the city's East End.

He looked down at his calf-length cargo pants – khaki was 'de rigeur', Loney's were apple green – and his Help for Heroes socks were now threatening to sink from the probing human eye into his trainers. The stinking, damp, all-pervasive fog got everywhere. He watched as the left sock did a 'Titanic' and he resigned himself to the inevitable blistered heel. But the Rev Peter Loney consoled himself with the righteous thought that he had at least spent his congregation's early Christmas gift of Primark vouchers to the tune of £15 well if not exactly wisely. His gratitude was now in plain view and would be appreciated even by wee Mrs Singleton who had been much put out for, as she had voiced very loudly, she had learned to knit socks on four needles at school. Loney had shown his appreciation of his church congregation's generosity by giving one and all his tips for that day's meeting at Kempton Park, thus removing the necessity of buying The Glasgow Morning News and perusing the third from back page as Loney's alter ego was 'Saddled', that newspaper's esteemed racing tipster. It crossed his mind that he should perhaps open the thin, blue envelope that had been slipped to him by the fog-shrouded figure just minutes before. After all, that was probably why he was there. When the trumpet sounded, Loney went. No questions asked. He eased his Rudolph sweatshirt – too big by two sizes but at three quid he had been unable to resist – cautiously away from his body with

The Ginger Bottle

his frozen, damp hands and felt the chill seep through him. Every piece of clothing was now soaked. He knew he had better read whatever the envelope contained fast before the ink spread and the meaning was lost forever. Slipping the blue sheet of paper out of the small envelope, Loney grinned. No chance of the ink running. Pencil. Written by a disciple of the tribe of Ikea, no doubt. He looked up a few seconds later and nodded to the gate-keeper further down as that man twirled his key in a rather large padlock, tested that the tall, blue gates opened then entered that hallowed ground. Loney waited until the man had vanished along one of the paths before following him in through the gates. He thoughtfully closed them behind him as he thrust the letter inside his trouser pocket.

The park official had now vanished which was too bad for he might have saved Loney some time. The letter, which, really, was no more than a note, had stated three things; a specified headstone he was to look at, examine the newly added information on it and to find out who had supplied the latest information. No, four things. He could use the fiver enclosed for out-of-pocket expenses. Loney glanced about him and was glad it was the Old Calton cemetery and not the Craigton of some of his forebears as that one was hilly and endless, definitely somewhere over the rainbow. Calton was or would be a joy; flat, definitely God's Little Acre, a mere three or four dozen headstones scattered at irregular intervals amidst serene lawns. Still, there were people lying beneath that well-kept grass, anonymous,

The Ginger Bottle

yet who had been grieved over just as sincerely in their day as those whose names at least had survived, deeply inscribed in granite of different hues and of different types of more humble stone. He knew that to track down his quarry, he would have to step lightly on the last resting places of his fellows and it disturbed his peace of mind a little. Now, what was he looking for? Red granite, humped-shaped and four feet high. He walked slowly along the path cutting a fine swathe through the heavy curtain of dank fog and grey silence, the traffic once more at a stand-still, he supposed. With granite, there was always a better chance of it remaining, more or less, intact. There was something infinitely sad about the ones weathered till no inscription now remained.

    The fog was now subtly lifting and the all-pervading gloom along with it. He was completely alone, hemmed in by the high walls along with the dead. And straight ahead was a headstone that appeared to fit the description he had been given. Loney gingerly stepped around the area where one of the martyred Calton weavers was interred and he could almost feel the eyes of the thousand mourners who had witnessed the interment that day boring into him. How had so many crammed themselves into such a small area, he wondered, and mentally vowed to find out more about that dreadful day. The names he had read as he had passed along, how many of them had in fact witnessed the troops firing on the striking weavers? How many of them had been related to those killed or wounded? He silently prayed that the McChesneys recorded in his note had

The Ginger Bottle

been some of them. At an intersections, Loney let his eyes roam as a new memorial loomed up through the fog like the prow of the Marie Celeste. A squared pillar topped by the image of a sea captain. When his heartbeat had eased off, Loney realised that it was inevitable that some connection would be with the sea with Calton being so near to the River Clyde. He skirted solemnly the last resting-place of the tea-clipper captain and wondered what sights and sounds that mariner must have experienced almost two hundred years before in continents Loney himself longed to visit.

The fog suddenly lifted and Loney spied a McChesney possibility fifty metres or so on his right. A sudden chill swept through his lean body and suddenly he wished he was anywhere on earth but in this Old Calton Burial Ground. Claws dug through his wet polyester sweatshirt and he knew that The Ginger Bottle must be open or Fat Face, his landlady's cat and property of that pub, would still be in the kitchen. He eased the black and white feline and its claws from his shoulders and placed it at the feet of the old sailor. He moved along steadily but the sudden squawking behind him told him that Fat Face was doing its best to add to the number of deceased bodies in that Little Acre. Lizzie Loudon overfed her pet which was just as well for it was the world's worst hunter.

Loney stood, notebook in his left hand, pencil behind his right ear and his right hand drying his specs still on his face with a damp hanky, the latter courtesy of Summer McNaughten, his would-be partner but not if Loney could help it. He made a sketch of the stone, stood back and muttered under his breath.

Loney whistled in amazement at the McChesney gravestone and looked back over at Captain McKinnon's. St Petersburg, Berlin, Paris. These people had travelled the world in their daily lives and yet it was all in a day's work to them. He thought back to when he had last gone beyond the Trongate at one end and Parkhead Cross at the other with the Calton stuck somewhere in between. A couple of miles! There and then he decided to do something about it. Walking the West Highland Way was out as he had vertigo just looking at it in the calendar in his vestry. But the Southern Upland Way was tailor-made for him. Bespoke, so to speak, with its great, gently rolling hills. A bit of illegal salmon poaching sounded irresistible but, as a Man of the Cloth, he knew that last bit was tempting but out. Maybe, though, salmon en croute in The Cringletie House Hotel, he dreamed, and then reality kicked in. That was it, a fish supper in Jedburgh. So be it! He looked again at the anonymous note and then at the gravestone. Back to the note. Typed on a computer with only a scrawled, probably disguised, signature at the bottom. 'A friend.' So, what had he been asked to do? Find out who had supplied the latest piece of information on that red granite headstone. His hand caressed the surface of the memorial. Granite was truly beautiful; cold, hard and smooth. His eyes travelled down to the last two lines, all bright gold and deeply incised. 'In loving memory of Norma

McChesney.' Not easy to accomplish. It must have been moved and then replaced. Still, his was a much easier task. MMV. Memorial sculptors always left their mark. He ignored the marks of the previous companies and noted only the most recent. As a local minister, he was well-acquainted with all the firms in the area. Not as many as there used to be, though, as cremation had slashed the number of burials but he knew the MMV premises in Cambuslang were almost opposite Tunnock's biscuit factory. Murdoch and Malcolm Vipond. If he visited them, he might manage to sneak into the factory and beg a few dozen boxes of teacakes for the Old Folks Christmas treat. Or, a quick phone call and job would be done. But it did not seem right to use the mobile here in the graveyard so he determined to do so on reaching the sanctuary of The Ginger Bottle. Up to his rooms, a quick change into dry clothes and then back down to his usual seat by the huge hearth, a still-used and appreciated relic of the pub's coaching days. Fat Face had already read his thoughts – that cat was an expert at reading body language, too – and was now scrambling over the wall on its way home to Lizzie.

Loney's rooms were above the main lounge of the old coaching inn and consisted of one sitting-room with a shelf for a kettle, a microwave and a toaster, one bedroom and a shower-room and toilet. He had no kitchen as such but all his meals were available to him in The Ginger Bottle at a reduced price. Breakfast, his favourite meal of the day, was always on the house as long as it was poached eggs

The Ginger Bottle

on toast or French toast. Duck eggs were poached once a month – a treat for the egg-addicted Loney.

He stepped out of the steamy shower-room and stood eyeing up his array of clean clothes, all hung neatly in an old, very old, oak wardrobe. The solid oak floor complimented the aged piece of furniture and, for a moment, he wondered how many powdered wigs and frock-coats it must have held during its very useful life. His sitting-room faced onto Abercromby Street itself and once dressed, he stood momentarily at the window and mulled over what he had achieved so far that dank, foggy morning. It did not amount to much. He had looked at a headstone and pocketed a fiver. The fiver he slipped into his church diary, wrote a few words of explanation before snapping on the elastic band that conveniently held it firmly shut. From his quick glance out of the window, he had learned one thing; no need now to use the mobile although, in all honesty, and Loney was a very honest man, he had been in no rush to do that. In fact, as the dead were, generally speaking, going precisely nowhere, he had relegated that piece of business to the following week, as a visit to the Viponds could be lumped together with a visit to the Tunnock's factory and a plea for the aforementioned boxes of not only teacakes but also caramel wafers for the Christmas party and Burns Supper. Mobiles were so impersonal and Loney was the hands-on type.

Locking his door, he made his way down the old winding staircase and let himself into the bar which was already filled with locals and made his way to the padded settle that was his by custom and booked with his usual quota of newspapers. He watched as the man who had made the phone call and Tunnock's visit unnecessary entered the public bar of that ancient hostelry. Three hundred years old and counting, The Ginger Bottle was an anomaly in the teeming city street but its future was safe as Glasgow's councillors were now less inclined to rip apart the city's heritage in return for the patronage of thousands of tourists who preferred the old coaching inn to the science tower that seldom worked. A couple of photographs outside, then a quick soup and sandwich meal inside could easily be fitted into a tour of Glasgow and the nearby People's Palace Museum.

"Murdy!" Murdoch Vipond knew where to look having recognised the voice as soon as he had entered the pub. He nodded over to Loney, signalled to the barman and then made his way across the room to ease his limbs onto the settle beside Loney. The warmth of the spitting logs eased every inch of his sturdy body and especially his aching bones.

"Bridgid's wedding?" Loney suggested. The monumental sculptor nodded wryly.

"Aye, Gary, I'm getting past that sort of thing but me and the wife had hired the band until 2.30am so, as the father of the bride, I had to stagger on, and I mean stagger, to get my money's worth. Something up?" he asked.

"Not at all." Loney waited until the new barman had slurped the pint glass's contents over the table before continuing. "Just need a bit of information, that's all.

Was about to phone you then I saw you cross the street."

"I've a business appointment but after that accident down the street at the lights, I thought a glass or two would steady my nerves. This city's populated by a bunch of eejits whose disregard for the law that says if you chuck yourself under a bus, your lifespan stands a fair chance of being extremely limited, is a constant puzzle to me."

"I've lost count of the times I've seen misses and near-misses," said Loney signalling for some tea and toast.

"Same here. Anyway, minister, what's the problem?"

"Two-fold, Murdy, and the answers are very simple. No need to phone a friend."

"Good, for my brain's on a par with my mobility right now. So, let's have it." Murdy had a good draw at his pint and then leaned back on the settle.

"It's about a headstone you worked on probably fairly recently as the inscription looks new."

"Where?" Murdy took another draught of his orange juice.

"Down the road, the Old Calton graveyard." Murdy shook his head and glowered at the orange juice.

"Not us, Gary. That one's been closed since the 1870s." This time it was Loney's turn to shake his head.

"Your firm's initials are on it right down at the bottom right-hand corner – on the reverse side, of course." But Murdy continued shaking his head.

"Anything in this neck of the woods is either Janefield or St Peter's these days. Very strange, though, about the initials." He looked at Loney and shrugged.

"MMV, that's what it says," said Loney.

"I can assure you that it wasn't us. The latest thing we're into is two feet high headstones that folk order for garden memorials when their loved-ones have been cremated and their ashes buried in their own gardens, still in the poly-bag. Comparatively neat, cheap and something that can easily be transported when the bereaved flit. It also gives the weans something to aim at when kicking a ball about and saves having to replace the next-door neighbour's fence constantly. Here's my card." Murdy slipped it along the table to Loney through a pool of fresh orange juice. Loney took it, dried it off and placed it in his diary. He was now not so certain that there was a quick resolution to his problem. He poured the now delivered tea into a slender porcelain cup and once again appreciated the pouring qualities of the small tea-pot. The milk was UHT but he had no objection to that.

"Can't see the point of someone doing a first-rate job on an expensive material headstone, granite, and not putting the right firm's name on it," he said, "for it makes no sense."

"Agreed. What was the family name?"

"McChesney." Murdy looked into the far distance before proclaiming,

"Rings no bells whatsoever. Maybe a very distant one but definitely not recently. We can ask Malky, if you want confirmation, Gary. I've sent him a text telling him to meet me here. We're due at Janefield to do a few bits of business. That winter vomiting bug has been a big boost to our business. McChesney? Not one of our regulars. But why the interest?"

"It's just someone asking me to look it over and make sure it's A1 workmanship."

"And is it?" asked Murdy curiously. Loney smiled and nodded.

"Perfection in itself, Murdy."

"So, if you're happy with it, why the query?" Loney proceeded to lie with disturbing ease for a minister.

"I've lost the address to write back to. A distant relative probably."

"Who knew that your word was your bond," said Murdy frankly. Loney wisely kept his head over the teapot as he topped up his cup. "Here's Malky." Murdy Vipond raised his voice as his brother appeared and slipped into the chair on the opposite side of the table. He shook his head when offered a drink.

"Just taken another appointment at Janefield so time is now at a premium, Murdy. How are things, Gary?" he asked.

"So-so, Malky. There's just a little problem I've been paid to solve and I've run up against a brick wall."

"Explain!"

"I've had a look at a gravestone in the Calton Burial Ground. It's been added to recently and has your firm's logo on it, so to speak, on it. The trouble is that Murdy says you didn't do it."

"McChesney? We did. Drink up, Murdy, mate."

"What? When?" asked his older brother in surprise.

"Three weeks ago. That stag weekend that went into six days when you and another few guys were stuck on the Bosphorus and banged up when you returned to shore." Murdy waved that bit of embarrassing news away as fast as he could.

"Just a bit of trouble with a few officials being overly officious, Gary," he explained hurriedly. "But more to the point, I don't remember any business being immediately outstanding concerning work in the Calton."

"That's because it wasn't outstanding. Just landed on the desk one day ordering a few lines to be added to a particular headstone. Cash enclosed. Paid for your bail. Got permission to move it on a very temporary basis, did the job at the workshop, replaced it and put the cash in the bank. All above board. We couldn't send a receipt for there was no forwarding address. It's still in the book. I assumed that the person was not local but would send for the receipt once they had checked on the work done. Now let's keep the cash coming in, Murdy boy, for Janefield awaits."

"Another brick wall, then," said Loney resignedly.

"Better than a double-decker bus, Reverend Loney," said the young barman with the shaky hands, edging in to clear the pint glass away and wipe down Murdy's half of the table. "Rhys Ronaldson's just clocked out."

"What happened?" Loney's face was a decided shade of pale now.

"Threw himself under a bus so they say. Maybe," he added.

"That was the one I was telling you about, the accident further down the street," said Murdy, his own ashen look returning. Loney did not look too good either. Rhys Ronaldson, the boy from the fog had died shortly after delivering that message. Nobody could miss knowing that that figure had been Rhys, his nephew Jojohn's best mate.
"He didn't throw himself under, Uncle Gary. He was pushed!" Loney looked in horror as his nephew suddenly appeared, then collapsed into the chair beside Malky.

Chapter 2

Kenna Duguid, formerly Loney, the Reverend Loney's former sister-in law, glanced briefly at the envelope she held in her right hand and sighed, not for the first time, in the last ten minutes. Her eyes were drawn once more to the scene in the street below. She sighed yet again, laid the letter down carefully on the small breakfast table that fitted neatly into the marginally wider bay window area of the tiny flat and then threw open the double-glazed window.

"What is it?" she asked of the woman on the pavement below. The answer had begun even before she had finished asking the question.

"It's the lollipop man," proclaimed the woman looking up at her.

"So which part of his anatomy had been punted by a bus or lorry this time?" Kenna glanced further up the hill of Abercromby Street towards the primary school.

"His feet and his lollipop. The janny says the council will sue the victim for damages as he was throwing the lollipop up in the air at the time, entertaining the kids. I said we'd run a fundraiser, a tea-dance, for his legal expenses. I thought of crowdfunding but that's too boring and too much like begging in my opinion. Are you game?"

"Aye." Kenna slammed the window shut. She smiled. The elusive lollipop man would be bedridden for a while and that suited Kenna down to the ground. His memory was second to none and that might just come in handy. That and The Ginger Bottle pub being inaccessible to him would make sure he was on top of his game. Failing, that of course, there was always Auld Dan McNab. Kenna opened the window once more and shivered as the cold blast hit her yet again. "Bessie!" The woman below on the pavement looked up as did the two women she was now talking to. "Is he in the hospital?" The lollipop man was a fine actor and it was just as well to make sure.

"Saw him into the ambulance myself. The Royal. Toes and lollipop both crushed, said the lassie paramedic. I heard her tell her mate." That was much better, more reliable than just Bessie second guessing. "Let me know when he can have visitors and here's a tenner for a box of Thorntons – coffee creams are his favourites." She watched the ten pound note float slowly down on the still, dank air then Kenna closed the window on all further chat and eyed the letter again. She slipped out the sheet of cheap, blue, lined paper from the thin, blue envelope and read it over again slowly and thoughtfully. 'An old neighbour of my mother's thought I might be interested. She wrote to me – I'm afraid that letter is God only knows where – telling me that Norma McChesney's death is recorded on the family gravestone in Old Calton Burial Ground." But that graveyard hasn't been used in well over a hundred years, thought Kenna yet again. But maybe it had just been inscribed on an old stone. Maybe the woman had died abroad and wanted to have her name written down among her ancestors. Nothing unusual in that. But why did the old neighbour think someone around here would be interested? Why did someone actually think Kenna would be interested? She looked again at the names already down on that mysterious headstone and shook her head. None of them rang any bells. Should they mean something to her? She looked at the £5 note that was in the envelope. What was she supposed to do? Check that it was done properly. That's all it said. But then what? Who were these people? Kenna slipped a few chips into her mouth and took a long sip of tea from her favourite mug. The tea was strong and the milk sour. It made no difference to her as she did not like milk anyway. She finished it in two gulps and then replaced the china mug on the tray beside the soggy box. Tully the cat next door was a sort of nouvelle cuisine cat. He preferred his potatoes in roasted goose fat for they reminded him, Kenna suspected, of his cannibal days when his feathered friends were fair game. Lifting her short, leather jacket from the back of a chair, she sauntered out of the flat, letter and purse in her extremely large bag, fish in paper in her hand. Tully's owner gratefully received the haddock, abandoned her turn at sweeping the stairs and quickly made for the kitchen; a buttered roll and a little bit of fish on it with a cup of tea and the rest of it in Tully's 'I'm the Boss' bowl made her day.

Kenna moved from the damp air off the street and into the hot air of the
hairdressing salon. The door jammed as she tried to close it behind her. The notice stuck to the glass in it claimed her attention.
'As an eco-friendly business, Killer Kuts does not sell plastic Rain-Mates. Please do not embarrass the

staff by asking and thus avoid a refusal.' Josie Duguid, the owner of the establishment, had added to it in an orange highlighter, 'But Shug's Surplus Sundries does up the lane." The loud chatter competing with even louder hairdryers assaulted her eardrums and assured Kenna that her mother's business was doing really well. A quick look round the small shop told Kenna that her mother was through the back; a small gents' hairdressing chair cum kitchen/staff base and a large mirror. Josie was Auld Dan's preferred hair stylist. Rumour had it that he had been thinking of forsaking his loyalty to Brother Cadfael and was now almost ready to embrace fully a Prince William all or nothing. Room was at a premium and Kenna had to squeeze her way past chairs and trendy hairstylists to reach the gents' salon. These days, Josie specialised mainly in the pensioners of both sexes and left the money-making part to her assistants.

The large mirror above the small basin showed Dan sitting in the large faux-leather chair closely scrutinising the contents of his free coffee – Asda's own make – in the mug in his hand while Josie did the necessary.

"This UHT?" asked Dan peering still further into the small mug.

"Naw!" All conversation back here was strictly limited. Kenna leaned with her back against the mirror and faced Dan.

"How's the food and the insurance claim, Dan?" she asked.

"Hurting in both cases. I'm in here to get a makeover. I want a new direction in my life that doesn't include weans, lollipops of the massive variety and no-win, no-fee lawyers. The very best of luck to my recently injured friend and successor."

"Well, let me take your mind off it all, Dan," she said. "A stroll down memory lane minus all three of the afore-mentioned categories. Does the name McChesney ring any bells?" Dan gave it his best shot after several minutes of deep thought.

"The circus ones who married into another circus family, Kenna? That the one?" he asked, obviously curious.

"Could be. I know nothing about them except for the names on a headstone."

"Red granite? Old Calton burial ground? Just down the road?"

"That's the one."

"I've seen it. Now that's a very uncommon name around here. I think they've all moved on, years ago, in fact. Either died or emigrated probably." Dan took a hesitant sip of coffee and seemed quite satisfied. "Any wee ginger biscuits, Josie?" he asked hopefully.

"Naw!" That reply seemed to be no more than was expected.

"The McChesneys, Dan, anything at all come to mind?" Kenna waited patiently.

"Aye, but what's this all about?" he asked glancing round her form at the mirror. He seemed quite satisfied at his new hairdo. Josie drew him a sinker and he quickly remembered she had charged him full price the last time and there was no way he was foregoing his OAP discount today. He gave Josie a smile in the mirror and Kenna his full attention as she was, after all, that hairdresser's daughter. Kenna drew the sheet of cheap, flimsy writing-paper from the depths of her enormous shoulder-bag. Dan laughed.

"Like airmail paper. God, I haven't seen that in decades. Everybody used it in my young days. Very light, saved money on the postage, that and an aerogramme. Email knocked that on the head. But you're going back a bit, Kenna. Did you know that Gary Loney got one like it left for him in The Ginger Bottle last night. Are you doing family history? That an old letter?"

"Not at all, Dan. I just received this a few days ago. I'll read it aloud to you as Ma might have her design spoiled if you move your head – again!" Kenna could be a real nippy sweetie and Dan knew it. She read the part she thought absolutely necessary to evoke an answer she required and waited while her mother clipped away and Dan turned back the years.

"That brings back memories right enough. That McChesney family's long gone. You see, hen, that lassie, Norma McChesney, was a McChesney right enough but the family itself that brought her up were cousins. Her da was the only son, the rest were all daughters. His name was Hugh McChesney, but he died young, him and his wife. TB and their only child, Norma, was just taken in by the Coulters, her mother's family. Cousins, you see. She was lovely looking, but very quiet, mousy in her ways, a very pleasant girl." Auld Dan was now back in the past. Kenna was pleased for it might mean she would have no need to see the most recent lollipop man in hospital.

"So, what happened to her?" asked Kenna. Dan just shrugged thoughtfully and squinted again at the mirror. He seemed quite hopeful.

"Who knows? Hopped it to America with a ne'er-do-well boyfriend, one Leonard Wylie by name. Actually, he'd been orphaned in a way, too. His folks had left him one day with his granny to go to the pictures and then hopped it to Skegness. Worked in Butlin's, I think. Anyway, it was the old, old story. Opposites attract. Do you remember the fuss, Josie?" Josie shook her head and kept cutting. "Right enough, that would have been the time you were living in Perth with your granny. Aye, I remember now. Your granda, Josie, had tried, unsuccessfully, to outrun a train and your ma sent you and wee Ellen to Perth to keep your granny company for a few years."

"Six, to be exact," said Josie sourly. "The guys there were only up for running away as far as the local working-men's club." Kenna tried hard not to laugh and get thrown out.

"Anyway, Kenna, why did the person who wrote the letter think you might be interested?" asked Dan. Both Dan and Josie looked at Kenna and waited for her reply.

"I've no idea. I've done a fair bit of family history, as Ma knows, but there were no McChesneys in our family tree."

"And I can't recall anybody mentioning that name lately," said Josie. "Want some tea?" Kenna shook her head and folded the sheet of paper.
"It was a big thing round here at the time," said Dan, "but it all went quiet when Norma wrote and explained that love conquers all and New York was heaven on earth. A neighbour's son in the Merchant Navy met up with them in Central Park and everything fizzled out after that. She was only a cousin, after all."
"Well, Dan," said Kenna, "somebody's paid for another line or two on that red granite headstone." Dan shook his head and got a slap from his hairdresser in return.
"Sounds like the kind of thing an American would do. Touching base, as they would say." Dan was well up in the modern lingo – he thought.
"All done, sir," said Josie sarcastically, her hand held out for her money.
"Want a lift back to the sheltered housing zone?" asked Kenna. Dan shook his head in reply and showered the other two in cut hairs.
"No thanks, Kenna. Nice job," he said squinting again into the mirror. "Think I'll buy a paper and then hirple back up to The Ginger Bottle and catch up with my cronies."
"If anything about the McChesneys comes to mind, let me know and I'll stand you a pint – if it's any good. This will annoy me till I get to the bottom of it."
"You could always write back to the sender and have it explained a bit more," Dan suggested as he

wrapped a huge fleece scarf round his neck and put his cap back on.
"No address. It was probably on the original envelope. Still, I don't suppose it's of any importance. Take care and mind how you go."

Kenna closed the door firmly behind her. The smell of the dank fog still lingered in the air although a dismal greyness had somehow managed to dispel most of it.

Abercromby Street was extremely busy right then, the traffic piling up as the police coped with the scene of the accident. Nothing new there. She decided that the writer of the letter was correct in thinking her interest in the information regarding the newly inscribed headstone might just be minimal. It was now non-existent. And yet. She sighed heavily and loudly. The traffic on her side of the street began moving. The opposite side was
devoid of traffic, the police allowing no traffic to use it. The bus in front of her moved off and The Ginger Bottle appeared in all its 18th Century glory. It occupied a building whose origins were now lost in the mists of time along with the documents telling who had originally owned the building. That prolonged squabble had saved it from official oblivion and frequent acts of vandalism over the 20th Century, all in the name of civic
 improvements. It looked exactly what its original purpose had been, a coaching inn. Time and progress had touched it only inasmuch as sanitation and electricity had surreptitiously and reluctantly bowed to local byelaws and insurance claims caused by

falling candles. A high standard of basic food and low standard of service appealed to those whose main aim was to be assured that they got exactly what was expected – a quality pie and a pint. The Ginger Bottle was the comfort zone of a large, varied and loyal, not to say grateful, clientele. The sign hung limp and still in the very cold air. The traffic halted once more and Kenna's natural curiosity prevailed. There was something behind that seemingly innocent letter. She moved off the pavement and crossed over the street. She knew that Gary Loney's circle of friends and acquaintances was wide and varied and that he would be occupying, right then, his seat in The Ginger Bottle as usual. His evangelical calling was supplemented by his job on the side as The Glasgow Morning News's racing tipster. Kenna knew that he had never been any nearer a horse of any description other than the police ones that occasionally strolled with disdain and shit along the entire length of Abercromby Street as he sat holding court in the pub. Loney had an encyclopaedic brain and the fact that he was that swine of an ex-husband of hers' brother, did not diminish her regard for him.

Kenna turned the brass knob and heard the bell tinkling, a sound that had been heard by legions of customers down the centuries. There was a certain thrill in that thought.
"What the hell are you doing here? Get back to work right now!" she yelled across the lounge-bar without waiting for an answer to her question. A figure rushed past her and out of the door. This time the mellow jangling was lost in Kenna's annoyance as

The Ginger Bottle

she strode over to Loney. "You know he should be working! Are you encouraging him to skive off?"
Loney indicated the empty seat across from him and Kenna sat down heavily, her eyes filled with fury. "My mother pays him good money to work not sit in this pub and natter."
"Jojohn has never skived a minute in his life. Your son is very upset and he came to me for a bit of comfort as his best pal has just been crushed to death by a bus. What you should be asking yourself is why he came to me, his uncle, instead of to his mother who lives just across the street." Kenna rose again. "That's right, avoid the big question. Still, I'll apologise right now if you're going after him," said Loney eyeing her blandly. Kenna sat down again.
"What's bothering him really?" she asked and Loney just shook his head.
"I've just told you. He's just seen his best friend die before his eyes. What part of that do you not understand?"
"Which pal?" she asked, footering in her bag.
"Does that actually matter?" Kenna was way down his list of decent human beings and she knew it. Loney was not very high on her list either and he knew it but did not care. That was the difference that irked Kenna. He lifted his newspaper. "Goodbye."
"I've a puzzle you might like to solve," she said, dismissing the previous conversation from her mind as she took the sheet of paper out of her bag. Loney knew immediately what had happened.
"Not interested."

The Ginger Bottle

"Liar!" Loney folded the newspaper in his hand and finished his tea. Kenna Duguid was a very complex person and Loney wondered why his brother had been foolish enough to think that that made her interesting enough to marry. Nether of them was suitable for any sort of partnership.

"All right," he said, "what would you like to know about the McChesney headstone?" Loney was a showman at heart and he laughed as a look of surprise flitted like a comet across Kenna's hazel eyes. The face, as usual, remained stern, carved out of ice.

"Everything you know."

"Red granite and the words, which I presume are in your letter, recently inscribed on it by an unknown monumental sculptor. The firm's logo, so to speak, MMV, is on it and they know nothing of who requested it. A letter plus instructions plus cash appeared on their desk. No address, all evidently above board. Here endeth the lesson. No questions are permitted. Your turn." Kenna regarded him askance then looked at the letter in her hand.

"And what exactly was written in the letter you obviously received?" She never beat about the bush. Loney looked up from the newspaper again and began jotting in his notebook again. The interview was now at an end. Kenna left The Ginger Bottle.

Loney perused what he had just written.

Item 1; Why had he and Kenna been chosen to receive those letters?

Item 2; Who could predict a joint effort?

The Ginger Bottle

Item 3; Why had Kenna come straight to him and had not first checked the headstone?
Item 4; What had she actually investigated if anything?
Item 5; Who might have been able to furnish her with the information she was probably withholding from him for her ability to share was zero? She was all take and no give in every area of her life excluding moggy needs.

Loney now had an overwhelming desire to solve this puzzle. It was not a Mensa job but it intrigued him just the same. He sat where he was and waited for Jojohn to come back. He did not have long to wait.

Jojohn had always been a kid who had gone all round the houses before getting anywhere near the point he was intent on making. Loney resisted the temptation to concentrate on his predictions for meeting at Ayr. There was nothing like a few minutes in Kenna Duguid's company to remind you how close a human being could come to being a sub-human mess. Jojohn had his full attention as the boy's mind roved all over the place except the junction of Abercromby Street and London Road.

"You know I've brought in a lot of clients to Killer Kuts, Uncle Gary." Loney nodded in agreement.

"So I've been told. That salon's a gold-mine, they tell me."

"That's just since I started, since I finished my course." Loney smiled at his nephew's simple honesty.

"Just required a modern take."

"And a change of name," said Jojohn. "'Permutation' was brilliant – in the Sixties," Jojohn added, "but right now it's for the over-sixties, maybe even for the over-eighties. Nothing wrong with that, of course, for they're great payers, these old folks. Cash on the nail."

"Just that it doesn't actually challenge your creativity, is that it, Jojohn?" said Loney.

"That's it exactly. You're the creative type yourself. I've heard some of your speeches, I mean sermons, up the top of the street. Saw you being bundled into that police van. No need for the rough stuff, I thought." Loney waved that thought away.

"Just the lads giving me a lift home, Jojohn." Loney was not quite sure about the 'creative' bit. He distinctly remembered being very rattled that day about something which he now could not even remember.

"Anyway, young folks pay through the nose for a stylish cut these days and it doesn't take them three months to make a return appointment. They don't have to wait until the perm grows out. Granny's offered me a partnership. She doesn't want to retire as she says perms will definitely make a comeback with the male clientele. She's concentrating on the modern version of short back and sides these days and does it very well. I've saved quite a bit over the years and a loan might just do the trick. Right now, I'm thinking it over. I don't want to sound too keen even if she is my granny." Jojohn suddenly wiped his eyes with the back of his hand. "Rhys was my sounding-board." Jojohn finally broke down.

The Ginger Bottle

"What actually happened this morning, Jojohn?" Jojohn took a deep breath before beginning.

"It was dark as well as that heavy fog and I'd just turned into Abercromby Street. I'd walked about fifty metres on this side in this direction when somebody shouted, "Grab him!" Next thing this figure, black tracksuit, hoodie, loomed up out of the fog from amongst all the folk on the pavement. He was dodging through them and it was all over in a second. I just tripped him up and he staggered against me, bounced off a wheelie bin at the edge of the pavement and then fell sideways into the street and under a bus." Now that Jojohn had begun, he could not stop. "I turned away, couldn't face it and then I heard him cry out and knew it was Rhys. That was his final breath. I killed him." Loney could almost feel the panic rising in his young nephew.

"No, you didn't, it was a terrible accident. Take a drink of that sparkling water from the bottle there."

"If I hadn't tripped him, he'd be alive right now."

"Listen to me, Jojohn, the person who put out the wheelie bin is probably saying the same sort of thing right now. He or she'll be saying that if they hadn't put that bin in that particular spot, young Rhys would still be with us. The police are saying, I'm told, that Rhys hadn't even been in the newsagents, he wasn't the shoplifter. Wrong place at the wrong time. The police are treating it as a dreadful accident."

"Rhys didn't think so. He didn't forgive me," said Jojohn his head in his hands, his voice now coming in gulps.

"Now how could you possibly know that?"

"Because he shouted 'Tell Loney to watch out!'"
"He was just saying that it wasn't your fault," said Jojohn's uncle putting his arm round his nephew's shoulder. But Loney's thoughts were elsewhere for Jojohn had never been known as Loney. He had been Jojohn Duguid all his young life as Kenna had decided to jettison Robert Loney the day her son was born. Yes, Loney, Gary Loney, would certainly be watching out from now on.

Chapter 3

Loney watched as Josie Duguid walked slowly with her grandson down towards the scene of the accident on the pavement opposite him. Jojohn clutched the small bunch of flowers with one hand and his granny's arm with the other. Josie patted his hand and whispered to him. Jojohn nodded and attempted to straighten up. Failing miserably, Josie put a comforting arm around his shoulders. Loney wondered where Kenna was until a slight movement caught his attention and he recognised Kenna's form just inside the graveyard gates. She was leaning against one of them, on the phone, her back to the street and her son. Loney watched her for several minutes. She would never change. Josie had brought up the boy. Kenna's interests had always been elsewhere.

A sudden scream rent the air and Loney saw Jojohn race back up the street, flowers still firmly clutched in his hand. Loney quickly intercepted him and steered him gently but firmly in through The Ginger Bottle and up to the privacy of Loney's own rooms. Back in Abercromby Street, Josie carefully avoided the spray from the hose held by the man noisily flushing the blood away as she placed her own bunch of winter blooms against the soaring grey column of the street light. She glared across at her daughter, sighed, and then walked back to Killer Kuts.

Jojohn wept noisily and wiped his nose and his eyes with the palms of his hands. The flowers were now settled in a vase and the cellophane binned.

The Ginger Bottle

Loney placed a mug of microwaveable Bovril on the coffee table in front of his nephew.
"It'll have cooled by the time you've finished washing your hands and face." Loney's phone went off and Jojohn headed for the shower-room. "He's alright, Josie." That was it. The Duguid women were not addicted to long speeches. Jojohn reappeared, his face pale, eyes red, hair immaculate. He had always been very particular about his appearance and Loney smiled slightly as the boy absently brushed some of the leaves from the flowers off his coat. He burst into tears again and Loney pressed him firmly onto the sofa.
"You can eat with your coat on or off but as it's Bovril and with the condition you're in, the first stop after here will likely be the dry cleaners." Jojohn took the hint and stood up. Loney hung the coat up on a wooden hanger behind the bedroom door. There was something about Jojohn's preferred drink – water – that he doubted was likely to bring warmth and comfort to the boy and Loney's kettle only worked in fits and starts. Jojohn drank the Bovril between heartfelt sobs.
"It was the sight of Rhys's life's blood being flushed down that drain."
"Shook me a bit, too, I must admit, Jojohn."
"Bad timing. He was my best mate, Uncle Gary. He always helped me carry all my equipment when I was involved in competitions."
"Probably fancied the chance to view the girls really close up." Jojohn reluctantly nodded in agreement.

The Ginger Bottle

"I wonder why he was running. An appointment?" Jojohn looked closely at the bread that Loney had placed beside the soup on a small tray. "That stuff's stale." Loney took no notice.

"Somehow I don't think he was going for an interview. Out of character, I think." But Jojohn shook his head emphatically.

"You didn't know him like I did, Uncle Gary. I think he had a definite idea of where he wanted his career to go."

"What career?"

"Communications. Big field, massive opportunities. A bit of fetching and carrying initially, of course, but once he'd proved his versatility, he was bound to be snapped up." Loney wondered how his naïve nephew would ever survive in the cut-throat world of style and fashion.

"It's too late for all that now, Jojohn, so if you're finished, we can go downstairs and have a chat in the warmth. The heating engineer's due tomorrow and then, maybe, this flat's temperature will cease resembling that of the top of Mount Everest." Jojohn put his coat back on and automatically checked his appearance in the mirror.

"Think the street will be clear?" he asked. Loney nodded. Jojohn still looked very pale as he glanced at the flowers.

"I'll place them there for you later. I expect your granny will have already done that with hers, so I'll make sure they're together. I'll tie them to a lamppost with a bit of string."

"Gardener's twine."

"Eh?" Loney retrieved the flowers and dried them off with a bit of kitchen paper.

"What you've just taken out of the drawer. Twine."

"Must remember that." Loney then cut what he considered to be a suitable length of what he now knew to be gardener's twine.

"I think you should go straight back to Killer Kuts once you've warmed up a bit. But you can come with me if you like," Loney suggested and was not surprised when the invitation was declined.

"I don't think so, not just yet. There be lots there – floral tributes, I mean."

"Jojohn, your mate was a feckless, work-avoiding, dozy git who was well-liked by all. That part of the pavement will be a no-go area for a while. I'll go and see his folks later on. This has been one bloody awful day and it's still only half-past twelve. Come on. Your granny will be worried about you and your clientele will be all over you giving you comfort and joy. Rhys Ronaldson would be well satisfied with that as his legacy to his best pal."

Lizzie Loudon was halfway up the stairs when Loney opened the door.

"Josie's just sent word she'll be over in ten minutes to fetch Jojohn." Lizzie smiled and gave Jojohn a hug before they all went downstairs.

The three of them entered the lounge-bar and Loney took possession of his customary corner. He motioned for Jojohn to sit opposite him. Lizzie disappeared.

"Before all this happened, Jojohn, when did you last see Rhys?"

"This morning. We were opening up the salon and Rhys stopped by. It was still really gloomy because of the mist, more like fog really. He always stopped by and asked if we needed milk or anything." His hands again hid his face and Loney waited until he had recovered.

"That's what mates do, help each other," Loney added softly. Jojohn shook his head slowly.

"No, he just fancied wee Elma. Anyway, we just had a word or two and then he headed down the street." Loney was puzzled. Somebody had given Rhys that letter but who?

"And that was the last you saw of him, was it?" asked Loney. Jojohn sighed deeply.

"More or less."

"Yes or no?" Loney waited.

"No," said Jojohn finally, "somebody stopped him and he crossed the street."

"I thought you could barely see across the street."

"See in detail. But I could just about make out the lamps shining very feebly above the door of this place, The Ginger Bottle. Somebody was waiting there. I was sweeping the pavement. It was just a very indefinite movement, that was all. Dark clothes, too dark to make him out."

"It was definitely a man, then?" Loney was taking nothing for granted.

"No, definitely not. Just somebody, a mere shadow. But maybe I just imagined it. I was anxious to get in out of the cold."

"How long did they speak for, Jojohn? Can you remember?" Jojohn shook his head.

The Ginger Bottle

"I don't know for the fog was thick and brown and blotted everything out." Could have been one of the pub's cleaners, thought Loney sourly.

"Was Rhys working for anybody on the quiet?" he asked. The boy thought long and hard.

"Difficult to tell for he could be very close-mouthed at times, even with me. He was always involved in something and I never asked. I heard a lot in the shop, of course, for he was well-liked by the girls." Being totally feckless probably came across to seventeen-year-olds as a free spirit, thumbing his nose at the world, thought Loney barely suppressing a smile.

"Any idea who he might have been helping out recently, Jojohn?" Loney felt that getting any real information out of his nephew was like driving a bus with the brakes on. Jojohn now had his deep-thinking look on his very pale face. Loney waited for a minute or two.

"He was running errands for Malky Vipond. Malky likes to wheel and deal a bit but only through external agencies." Loney's flagging attention had suddenly deepened.

"The monumental sculptor?" he asked.

"Aye, that's him. Maybe Mr Ronaldson will get a decent discount if they decide to bury Rhys and.." Jojohn's voice broke then tailed off.

"Don't think about it right now," said Loney quickly.

"If they don't, I'd like to commission some sort of memorial," stated Jojohn firmly and then broke down again. Loney waited.

"So, you do have savings?" Jojohn nodded vigorously.

"My granny always promised me that she would take me into the business as a minor partner to begin with. I've been saving all my life for that day. Yes, I've got some money put by." All nineteen years, thought Loney, and felt some kind of primeval emotion course through him. He coughed loudly. "Maybe Granny will wait." Jojohn looked at Loney hopefully. "Of course, she will."

"I've got £1906. Christmas and birthdays and that wee job I had at night in Tesco's have all bumped it up."

"Just wait and see. Let all the emotions die down first before making a big decision like that." Malky Vipond, thought Loney, now who would have thought of him? He had made the inscription and was now possibly the one who had given the letter meant for Loney himself to Rhys. He had certainly been in the area not long afterwards. Was there a connection after all? If it had been Malky, why had he not just spoken to Loney about it? But about what? There was a mystery there, it seemed, but what was it? The first communication had been a simple note telling Loney to wait by the graveyard gates that morning. He had thought it a prank but had waited nevertheless. Was somebody just having an expensive prank played out that involved Loney and Kenna? Somebody with a warped sense of humour? But why involve Loney? Why Kenna? Suddenly Jojohn shifted and sat right beside Loney on the settle.

The Ginger Bottle

The Ginger Bottle was crowded but space opened as it had for Moses at the Red Sea and Josie Duguid and her daughter Kenna strode along that deserted highway till both ladies loomed over Loney and his nephew. The gap soon vanished behind them as the pub's clientele resumed their busy lives and the emptying of their glasses. The Ginger Bottle's staff performed like a well-oiled machine, dispensing drink in jig-time and ejecting any potential trouble-makers with consummate ease and the minimum of fuss. Pies were the speciality of the house with macaroni ones a new and welcome addition to a somewhat restricted menu. Haggis ones were being flaunted as a delicacy making their debut in the next month or so as a nod to Scotland's National Bard. The pork and haggis links on a bap were the only exemption to pies, quiche and chips, having got the seal of approval from those followers of the Bard the past January when the haggis had exploded in the microwave and Aldi's sausages had saved the day and the OAPs' Burns Supper at lunchtime.

"Your granny here's going to take you to Perth for a few days, Jojohn," said Kenna, her eyes still on her mobile. "Hop it and pack a few things. They're very particular through there." Kenna glanced up at her son as she finished texting.

"I'm going to the funeral." Jojohn did not move an inch.

"Forget it! That shop's your granny's nest-egg and she can well do without a blubbering idiot embarrassing her clients over the next few weeks. You can go for long walks by the river and visit the odd museum and depress the exhibits instead." This was the caring side of Kenna, thought Loney generously.

"I want to go, to say cheerio to Rhys."

"You had a chance this morning and you blew it. Now you've already stated your desire to attend the funeral and it's been noted by me, your mother. I've dealt with it so now move."

"I'll keep you up to date, Jojohn. You'll be at it," said Loney firmly.

"Another Loney loudmouth. This is no business of yours, so shut up." Kenna's voice was loud and piercing and Lizzie came over from behind the bar.

"Out!" These two knew each other of old.

"Still selling the same old minging pies, I see," said Kenna but she rose none the less. "Right you, move!" Jojohn moved this time. The highway parted once more. Josie sat down.

"Lizzie, put a couple of your best minging pies – forget the macaroni ones – into a poly bag along with some crisps and Diet Coke – put in a few bottles of sparkling water as well. I've hired a car and Jojohn and I can eat as we go."

"I'll put in some cheese and tomato sandwiches and a flask of coffee for you, Josie. I think Jojohn's quite partial to that as well. I'll send it all over in a cardboard box to Killer Kuts directly."

"Thanks, that'll let me pick up the car before I pick up the boy."

"Is Jeannie still running that business in Perth? Jojohn can probably help her out and take his mind off things," Lizzie Loudon suggested.

"Aye, but I'll tell her to keep him to washing hair no' cutting it. His nerves are in a terrible state and I don't think he should be let loose with scissors. I'll stay overnight and make sure he settles in. Killer Kuts more or less runs itself anyway. I'll give Karen a ring before I go and she can fill in for me for a day or two. Thanks for your help, Gary." Gary Loney's face was like thunder.
"That daughter of yours is a waste of space. He's lucky he's got you, Josie." Loney occasionally spoke the absolute truth.
"And you, too. Kenna's been like that all her life." She shrugged, her weariness clearly etched in the greyness of her features.

Loney left the pub shortly after Josie. Somehow, he felt drawn to the Old Calton Burial Ground and that red granite headstone. The high gates swung to behind him and soon he was quite alone. He withdrew the letter from his pocket and read it again trying to understand the point of it all. All right, he had already done his bit, had found out who had been the monumental sculptor, Malky Vipond. Job done. The only real question raised in Loney's mind was what was he supposed to do with that information. Was the information supposed to trigger another line of thought that a curious-minded man like the Reverend Gary Loney would find hard to resist? He read the additional inscription aloud. 'In loving memory of Norma McChesney.'
"You got one, too, didn't you, minister?" Loney started slightly and flushed a little as Auld Dan rose up from behind a tribute to someone who had

evidently been a paragon of virtue. Those were certainly the days, he thought. "I call him 'The Heidie'." Dan pointed to the statue. "There he is, book in one hand and the other outstretched to slap some boy's lug - hard."
"You could be right, Dan, but I think that the outstretched hand means that he was a philosopher boring the local populace to death." Auld Dan laughed.
"Anyway, that table-top slab just next to him is my favourite spot for a bit of sunbathing on a hot day."
"Which this isn't," said Loney and waited. He was not disappointed.
"Quite so, but my injured foot needs resting every hundred steps or so and that filled the bill. So, back to square one. Did you get one too?" Loney laughed.
"I take it that I'm not the only one if you're referring to one concerning this headstone, Dan," said Loney.
"I think somebody's taking the mickey out of you and Kenna. What did yours say?" What had Loney to lose?
"Virtually nothing except what I've just read aloud."
"But it still managed to grab your attention?" Loney nodded and Dan sat down on the inscribed memorial.
"Whoever wrote it asked me to find out who had done the latest work on the stone. The problem is, or the intriguing part is, that once that bit of information was gathered, there were no instructions as to what I should do with what I had learned."
"Maybe it's a matchmaker. Maybe somebody's trying to bring you and Kenna together."
"She's my sister-in-law!"

The Ginger Bottle

"Mere words. So, what do you want to know about the McChesney girl?"
"I take it Kenna has already spoken to you about all this?"
"Aye, that she has. I have undergone cross-examination by that particular woman and it was not particularly pleasant. In a nutshell, the girl hopped it with a local lothario and they settled in America. Rumours abounded at the time as she was the last person everybody thought would do that and all the local girls whom the gigolo had left behind tore his character to bits, naturally. They even suggested that he had had his wicked way with her and then had done her in. Then a local merchant seaman saw them in New York from where she had sent her auntie some postcards and that was that. Ordinary, plain postcards but with New York stamps, or American anyway. My bet here is that somebody in the States is into family history and will turn up asking what you've found out. You're probably saving them a few pounds initially."
"So, what you're saying, Dan, is that her memory is now resting with her ancestors?" Auld Dan nodded sagely.
"The Yanks are right into family history. Norma was the last of the McChesneys round here."
"And Kenna knows this?" said Loney. Auld Dan nodded. "The whole thing seems totally pointless to me, Dan. There's no address here I can write to so that I can let the writer know about the inscription, that it was beautifully done, I mean."

The Ginger Bottle

"I would say that it was an oversight if it was just your letter but the same thing has happened in Kenna's. I sneaked a look but don't tell her." Loney nodded absently for he was suddenly struck by the idea that his part in all of this was being orchestrated by Kenna herself. So, what was she up to? A division of labour where only she knew the full meaning of it all? Was she trying to get his curiosity aroused and have him do the leg-work? She probably did not know about monumental sculptors incising their marks on headstones. Cremation had now almost made the need for commissioning headstones a thing of the past. Vandalism and insurance claims for accidents concerning toppling stones had almost reduced everything to token floral vases. But there was still the mystery of the person Rhys had spoken to outside The Ginger Bottle. Had it really been Malky Vipond? Why had Rhys not mentioned to Jojohn that he was passing a note to Jojohn's uncle? Suddenly Dan's voice cut into Loney's thoughts.

"Sorry, Dan, what was that?" he asked.

"Too cold to dally here, Reverend Loney. I'm on my way to the lunch club for a bowl of soup and a toasted sandwich. See you!"

"Just a second, Dan, did the Viponds have any connections with the McChesneys in the old days?"

"Cousins. It was the Viponds' cousins the Coulters Norma McChesney stayed with after both her parents died. She was an only one and the Coulters took her in. Malky was very cut up about it when she ran off. Seems he had high hopes of tying the knot there. But it was Murdoch who was her Number 1 guy until

Leonard Wylie came on the scene. Murdoch had a nervous breakdown. It was all a long time ago. Somebody's just having a laugh at your expense. Probably watching you and Kenna chasing old ghosts. Probably your own brother for he's a real bastard once his back's up." Suddenly a shout broke into the conversation.

"Mr Loney!" The attendant hurried over, black bin bag in one hand and a litter-picker in the other.

"What is it?" asked Loney quietly.

"Your father's dead!"

Chapter 4

"In the name of God, did Jackie leave the chip-pan on? Many's the time I've warned him about that, haven't I, Gary?" But Gary Loney was already heading fast for his father's flat in Atlanta Street. Auld Dan shook his head and slowly left the graveyard on his way to buy his paper and get his lunch. He would pop into Bella's Bakery and get the news from Bella herself. Probably was a chip-pan fire but he had not heard the sound of a fire engine. Anyway, he thought, if Bella didn't know, she must be dead herself.

The usual crowd littered the entrance to the newly-built sheltered housing complex as Loney hurried inside. The constable on guard by the entrance was a member of his church and he saluted as Loney passed inside.

"What I'd like to know is what that one's doing here," shouted Kenna to Loney, her eyes having briefly been directed to Loney as he entered the flat itself. He ignored her, squeezed Summer, and entered what was now an empty flat.

"We're engaged, Gary and I," explained Summer, "and that gives me certain rights."

"Where's Da?" asked Loney ignoring both women as he spoke.

"Pronounced dead and then taken away. That officer at the front entrance probably knows where." Kenna continued to text an unknown victim who had probably had the good sense to switch the mobile off.

"It's a known fact that thieves follow quickly in Death's wake.
"She's a human version of a death-watch beetle." Summer was young, sassy and appeared to have something akin to a death-wish herself. She suddenly found herself outside on the landing alone and Jackie Loney's door firmly closed behind her.
"That hurt!" Kenna had a very strong grip. Summer took herself off to the newly-opened wine bar cum bistro just beyond The Ginger Bottle and an early cocktail. Lizzie Loudon smiled sweetly at her as she passed the pub.
"They get their mini petite tarte au boeuf from the same artisan cooks we do. We call our larger version Scotch pies." The roar of several clapped-out motorbikes racing past put paid to that one-sided conversation.

Kenna stuffed the mobile into her voluminous bag, Loney leaned against the sink.
"What happened?" he asked, folding his arms across his chest.
"He fell down the stairs. What I'd like to know is why they put a guy with incipient dementia up the stairs in the first place. He hasn't been steady on his feet for years."
"Just keeping him away from the front door, I expect. He wasn't that bad anyway. Who found him, Kenna?" asked Loney.
"One of the home visitors. Actually, she tripped over him, had hysterics and is probably now on indefinite sick leave with PTSD. It was her screaming and kicking in all the doors of the downstairs flats that

alerted everybody to what had happened. If she'd just pressed that alarm round his neck, it would have brought help much quicker. Had the whole block reaching for the Warfarin."

"So, he was alive when she found him?" Kenna shrugged.

"Who knows? He was certainly dead when help arrived in the form of Nessie Rough's grand-daughter who's off the school with a bad case of the skitters at the moment. She heard the screams as she passed by with her granny. They were off to see Mary Poppins at the Forge. It's not bad, really. I prefer Julie Andrews' version myself. Anyway, that girl's got a certificate in first aid and saw Jackie's neck was broken straight off. She has already filled in the form for the Young Glasgow Hero of the Year award which comes with a prize of £50 plus lunch vouchers for four at any council museum cafe. Valid for six months, it is. She says she'll split the lunch vouchers between the People's Palace and the Riverside Museum as the attendants there are ultra-nice, her words not mine."

"Where's Robert? Has he been near?"

"He went with his da's body. Very cut up, he is. He asked me to hang about here until he comes back and to touch nothing. Swine! What's he insinuating? That's your older brother for you. If there's anything you want, you'd better take it now for that figure of moral degeneration, that ex-husband of mine, will be through this place like a shoal of piranha fish when he gets back. I'm sorry about Jackie, though. Fancy a cup of tea? Robert will be back only God knows when and there's a wee glass dish with some Blue Ribands on the table." Loney sat down after selecting two mugs from the drainer and putting coffee and milk into both. Silence reigned until Kenna filled the mugs with boiling water. In truth, he felt as if he was in shock. His father had always been around. His life had consisted of hard work, the telly and the bookies where the cost of his bets would not have kept a sparrow in food. He was not much of a drinker and had frowned not only on Loney's vocation, but also on his sacred seat in The Ginger Bottle. Neither was his son his favourite tipster. He had been pretty average all told, a quiet, kindly husband to his late wife and a concerned father to both his sons. Loney sipped at his coffee.

"I expect the police presence is just until the curious find something else to fill their time," said Loney, his hands wrapped round the mug, badly needing the warmth it exuded. Kenna frowned.

"About this McChesney business, let's swap letters," she suggested.

"More of a note, in my case," Loney said passing the blue paper across the table and picking up hers. He now found it exceedingly difficult to concentrate or even care.

"Any farther forward?" asked his erstwhile relation. Loney shook his head.

"Not one step," he said taking a large gulp of coffee.

"I expect we're asking ourselves the same questions. Why us? Who actually cares and what's triggered this? Is it all just a wind-up?" suggested Kenna frowning thoughtfully.

The Ginger Bottle

"I've got answers to none of these so, right now, I'm officially chucking it, packing it in, walking away." Kenna sneered as Loney spoke.

"Doing the Pontius Pilate bit, Reverend Loney?" she suggested. Loney looked straight at her before answering.

"As a Man of the Cloth, I've always thought that Pontius was just a victim of bad publicity."

"Think I'll have a word with Summer," said Kenna. "Could be 'Bugger off!"

"That's two," Loney pointed out as he rose. "Tell Robert I'll be in the church hall. Young Rhys's relatives will probably be there at some point as the funeral tea usually takes place days before the event in our small but enlightened circle. Brings folk up to date and curiosity and caring are both to the fore and satisfied. At any rate, I'll go and see his parents as soon as they're back home." Kenna nodded.

"I'll tell Robert when he comes in. If he wants something to eat, I'll send him round to Lizzie Loudmouth Loudon's and she can feed him at your expense. It seems Jackie's weekly shop was about due and I know that your brother's not into the butter beans and pasta that are lurking over there. The cupboard is almost bare. Coupled with the fact that Robert's always skint, you'll just have to bear the brunt of it. Either that or it's the foodbank for him. I'll drive him there. Anyway, if you're interested, here's my latest take on the McChesney riddle. Somebody's conscience is bothering him, her or them."

"About what? Nothing happened."

"Just my take on it for what it's worth," said Kenna biting into a Blue Riband. "Or, I think Malky Vipond has got somebody's back up and is trying to stitch him up. Remember, there's a big contract coming up with those proposed memorials to the industrial unrest about the same time as the martyrs and it's worth plenty for the firm of monumental sculptors that gets it. And I mean plenty. Seems he's been fingered as a definite maybe for the guy who gave young Rhys that note to you. Auld Dan, though, swears that he was the figure who had spoken last to the boy. He'd only been asking him to get his paper from the newsagents at the foot of the street as his feet were playing him up. You and I, Reverend Loney, are just famous for being nosey. Then again, maybe it's just a wind-up after all. If you got a fiver in your envelope, too, buy a baguette from Greggs." Loney stopped by the door of the flat.

"I'm off. Don't forget to say goodbye to my fiancée, Kenna." Loney had no idea Summer had hopped it. That piece of advice obviously irritated Kenna and Loney smiled briefly. But he made a mental note to put Summer on the back burner.

Loney's arm was outstretched and about to push open the church hall door when Dan's voice halted the action.

"Just going home to read my paper, minister. Changed my mind about the soup. Any tips for the gee-gees?" he asked hopefully.

"I'll get back to you on that one, Dan. I'm a bit pushed for time right now."

The Ginger Bottle

"Just trying to take your mind off it, Gary. I'll read your forecast for myself," said Dan, his paper neatly folded under his arm. "I'm running a bit late myself due to the fact that young Rhys, because of circumstances beyond his control I might add, failed to bring me my paper as arranged."

"I'm told it was your feet that stopped you collecting it yourself? Feeling any better?" Loney's mind had cleared instantly.

"According to that thing on my wrist which looks like a watch but isn't, I decided to give them a rest as this contraption said that I had walked thirty miles yesterday. Four pounds down the drain as I had only gone to The Ginger Bottle and back from my flat three times. Even I could work that out."

"Looks like that's cream-crackered, Dan," said Loney pointing to the offending monitor.

"That's the conclusion I've reluctantly come to. Had to get this paper myself."

"When did you hire Rhys's services?"

"This morning. I'd got as far as The Ginger Bottle then chucked it. The fog, my feet and my chest don't mix. Then I saw young Rhys and hired him. Actually, no money was involved. He was a nice young lad." Mystery solved, thought Loney, and suddenly he wanted to laugh out loud. But right then was not the time nor place.

"Dan, come on in for some tea and buttered scones."

"I'm not dressed to enter a house of bereavement, Rev Loney."

"It's only the church hall, Dan," coaxed Loney. Dan shook his head.

The Ginger Bottle

"I'll pay my respects at the boy's funeral and, of course, my pal Jackie's. This is a very sad day for this community so I'll put on a wee punt or two to relieve the emotional stress I'm feeling." Loney watched, touched, as Auld Dan sauntered away to the bookie's.

Loney stood just inside the door of the hall and felt again how lucky he was to be the minister of this small community. Most of his work was done with the homeless and he felt relieved that that was the congregation's own pet project. The voices, now muted, were giving expressions of genuine sorrow for the loss of a boy who had grown up amongst them. But unpalatable facts had to be tempered with faith and the solemnity of the moment was uplifted by fond and funny memories of the deceased. Tables were laden, tea was being poured from giant teapots and home-baking uplifted the spirits of all there as always. Loney did the rounds and for the first time realised that his position had altered and that he was now looking for comfort from his flock.

"I think your brother is looking for you, Mr Loney." Loney smiled at the elderly lady and turned to look at the newcomer standing by the door. He hurried forward and walked past his brother. He had seen that belligerent look before, many times. Robert Loney's ire was almost tangible.

"The vestry," he said firmly, opened the door and sat down at the desk. Robert Loney had no option but to follow if he wanted to speak to his brother.

"Right!" Confrontation was written all over Robert Loney.

The Ginger Bottle

"Close the door and keep your voice down."

"I'm here for your half of the funeral expenses."

That was it.

"You can't possibly know what that figure is," said Loney quietly.

"I've made an educated guess." Robert stood with a smirk on his face.

"It will wait until it's paid out of Da's estate. That's perfectly normal. They will send in a bill," said Loney and waited, for he was not stupid enough to think that would be it.

"Well, if you think I'm paying good money to feed the morons of the local betting shop, you're mistaken."

"I'm not thinking anything, Robert, except that our father's just suffered a horrible death and you're only interested in his money. It's too early to do anything. He lived on his meagre pension from the Council and his OAP one. That was all he had. Both stopped at whatever time the doctor put down as the time of death on the death certificate."

"I'm the eldest son by far, eldest anything actually and heir to everything."

"And you can have it all whether you're entitled to it or not. Will it all be sold, including the Blue Ribands, on Ebay or announced on a black-bordered postcard in Bella the Baker's artisan shop window?" Loney was beginning to feel really pissed-off.

"I'll have that in writing, the bit about assigning all your rights in Da's estate to me."

"Bog-off, Robert, come back when that good man has been reverently buried."

"And you've got your fee for the service?"

"No fees are charged for funerals. Now," But anymore vocalised friction came to an abrupt halt as Kenna breenged into the vestry.

"They told me I'd find the two of you in here and then handed me a mug of tea as they've now run out of cups and saucers. Rhys has proved to have been immensely popular. The side plate you see here consists of two egg mayo sandwiches, one shortbread finger, one square Rocky Road and a scone with strawberry jam, home-made. No charge. Now I'll start on the sandwiches while you two digest the following tasty bit. Your da, Jackie Loney, owned that flat, no mortgage, all his."

"Put that bloody piece of bread down and repeat that bit of nonsense," boomed Robert. "If you think that kind of false rumour you're spreading will stop me taking hold of his bankbook and household goods right now, you're mistaken. Apart from £48.29 written in his RBS bankbook which I have safely in my back pocket, Da was skint. He's got some nice bits of furniture and a few bits of jewellery but that's it." Robert suddenly swung round to face Loney. "Have you put her up to this? Are you two having a laugh at my expense?" Robert's face was puce with fury. Loney laughed and shrugged.

"All news to me, brother."

"Well, Kenna, you heard him say that the lot was mine, so if what you say is true, I'll be the richer for around £90000." Kenna laughed long and hard.

"Which you will undoubtedly donate to a good cause. I heard Gary say nothing of the kind about your inheritance. I've only just come up to you having

The Ginger Bottle

been rather occupied with choosing what was put on this lovely, little plate. Take my advice, Gary, and make him order the most expensive funeral ever seen in these parts; a carriage and four black-plumed horses and make the post-funeral tea a dinner in the Malmaison." Kenna broke off laughing to taste a piece of Rocky Road. "Awful sweet," she said devouring the lot.

"How do you know he owned that flat, Kenna?" asked Loney.

"I witnessed his signature and posted the form for him. The day it was all finally fixed up, he gave me a box of Black Magic and asked me to keep the information to myself."

"If you're angling for a reconciliation, you've had it," spat Robert with as much venom as he could muster. Kenna shook her head.

"I can assure you, Mr Robert Loney, dozy git and work-shy creep to boot, that nothing could be further from my mind. I'm here to give this reverend gentleman some information regarding a mutual acquaintance. You, Robert Loney, would be better off wondering why the police are wanting a word with you concerning a quarrel you had with your da just before he was found dead at the foot of the stairs. Did he trip or was he pushed? Intriguing, don't you think, Gary? Pity that moronic goat and I are divorced or I might have got a packet. Or can a criminal – sorry, should have said murderer – be barred from inheriting under these circumstances? This might just turn out to be your lucky day, Reverend Loney."

"I never touched him, never! For God's sake, he was my own father." Robert looked wildly at each of the other two in turn.

"Only according to your own mother and she had – like you – a roving eye, I hear." Loney sighed.

"That's enough, Kenna, there's no need to tarnish memories. Are the police really wanting a word with Robert?" he asked.

"Yes, they really are. They are treating it, for some reason or another, as a suspicious death. But don't worry, Robert, regardless of the outcome, you'll be as skint as ever."

"You wish! You are one, vile human being."

"Evidence, ex-husband, evidence," and with that, Kenna flourished a long, narrow, foolscap, envelope with Jackie Loney's name and address on it. "This, from Messrs Wilmore, Valentine and Brewster, is the late, lamented head of the Loney family's last will and testament, all above board and very, very legal. Just a copy you understand. Had to do something by way of tidying-up the flat while waiting for the deceased's eldest son to appear. Mr Jackie Loney also left a very substantial insurance policy. Added in at the bottom of the will, Gary."

"So, Gary and I share it?" asked Robert in a voice which was a queer mixture of anxiety, hope and despair.

"Now Robert, dear," said Kenna, "half of around £150000 is nothing to look glum about but zero is, I must admit. Your da and I had one thing in common, we both loathed you. Jackie left the lot to Jojohn."

Gary Loney laughed loud and long as Robert grabbed

the copy of the will and stormed out of the room with Kenna following, her face wreathed in smiles. Her mind was now definitely off the mystery of Norma McChesney.

Loney felt that every feeling he had had been violently abused as he entered the church hall once more. Wee Mrs Singleton thrust a cup of tea into his hand, a chocolate macaroon neatly concealed between the saucer and the side of the cup. He was heartily glad for Jojohn's great fortune and equally worried about the suspicious death scenario. The constable had swapped his policeman's uniform for the more sober suit of a church stalwart.

"Dreadful day, Gary. Can't believe they've both gone," he said quietly. "A right shocker and I feel very sorry for Jojohn. Those boys were always together. Still, I'm told Josie's taken charge of him."

"Neither Kenna nor Robert has given any thought to the boy, David," said Loney, "he might as well be an orphan."

"He's still got you and his granny." David Mintin bit into a jam scone.

"It'll put him right over the edge when he hears about his Granda Loney," said the minister whose flock seemed right then to be in death's firing-line.

"Joined at the hip, those two were." Loney nodded in agreement for his granda's flat was Jojohn's preferred sleeping quarters.

"I'll put him up at the flat when he gets back till he sorts himself out."

"Too bad the church flat's being refurbished, Gary. More room there." Loney was always aware that his congregation had a very liberal outlook regarding where he had opted to stay during the refurbishment. He was going to be very busy over the coming days and he just could not imagine how he could deal with two funerals, an estate battle and Summer wanting a ring. He simply concluded as he left that life was a complete bummer.

Chapter 5

Loney regarded the breakfast in front of him with enthusiasm. He should not, he knew that, but poached eggs on sourdough toast had become a favourite of late. He could have done without the sourdough but beggars can't be choosers and he was skint. There was a taste to it that he just could not take to. Plain bread, such stuff dreams were made of, especially the outsiders. He smiled up at Lizzie Loudon and duly gave her the thanks she deserved, and Fat Face one rasher of the bacon he coveted when his owner had retreated behind the bar once more. He put aside his notebook and racing forecast and polished off the meal, almost succeeding in suppressing the grimace the sourdough brought forth. The composition of that meal was the result of Lizzie's summer sojourn of two almost whole days in San Francisco. He had eventually succeeded in weaning her off the apricot jelly inserted in the thick slices of sourdough but that was about it. Loney polished it all off and drowned the taste in a huge cup of strong tea. Fat Face now sat beside him on the settle and slept, disregarding the sounds of laughter and friendly arguments going on around him. Loney then resumed making predictions regarding the runners and riders at Ayr before preparing to email them to his editor from his Ipad. The visit to Rhys's parents the previous evening had been heart-breaking; shocked into silence, no weeping, just that unnerving silence and concern for Jojohn, their son's best mate. There had been photos of the pair

The Ginger Bottle

everywhere and Loney had finally left feeling utterly helpless.

Fat Face's slinky, silent abandonment roused Loney from his nightmare and he looked up as Kenna sat down opposite him across the table and brought out her A4 pad.

"He's still in the jail," she said pertly. Her concern ranked with what she might just make for tea.

"At the police station helping the police with their inquiries is, I believe, the correct way to phrase it," said Loney, sighing deeply. Kenna shrugged as usual.

"Anyway, his latest girlfriend or lover – my God, what a disappointment she's in for – is outside the police station waiting for his release and the photographers to appear and give her fifteen seconds of fame only it'll never happen because he's a bloody ugly, bit-baldy nonentity. Who'd want his photo?"

"I, personally, thought that was all the rage, being bald, uncompromising virility on show." Loney kept a straight face under very difficult circumstances.

"So must she. He's just an unfaithful reprobate."

"You, Kenna, were the one who threw him out so that your hands-on preference could take his place after one year of wedded bliss," Loney reminded her.

"And that one was no better! But, to get back to the nitty-gritty, it seems like your brother's not about to walk anywhere either into his lover's arm or what I know he'd prefer, The Ginger Bottle."

"They'll string out the questioning so as to save face a little," said Loney hitting the send button on his Ipad. That would keep a good few thousand of Saddled's followers happy if not actually in clover.

The Ginger Bottle

"Pity they couldn't string it out for a few months," said Kenna tartly.

"Just taking him in for questioning alone in connection with his own father's death would be fatal to his reputation and future if, indeed, he was in possession of either of those. A lifetime of being a complete loser has not gone to waste. A comforting thought, isn't it?" Loney suggested. Kenna ignored this attempt at humour. "Does Jojohn know?" he asked.

"What do you think? He's alive and well and in Perth and well away from enjoying the dubious delights of filial responsibilities although if he had his da's tendencies as regards women, I'd have him back here in no time."

"Robert's all mouth and you know it, Kenna," said Loney slipping his Ipad into its posh, tweed cover – a present from Summer.

"Well, he certainly proved that yesterday morning for the whole block heard him threatening your da."

"There's no excuse for that but it's still a long way from actually harming someone," said Loney decisively.

"Murdering's the word I prefer." Loney definitely did not.

"No doubt Robert will be bawling and shouting about suing the police for compensation so that'll take his mind off the will and put it onto how much he might realistically expect. Sweet Fanny Adams as we both know or maybe a scant apology." Loney sat back and wondered where the cat was.

The Ginger Bottle

"I'll tell you what he'll get, absolutely nothing, for while you've been sitting here with Fat Face in The Ginger Bottle," But Loney chimed in suddenly with, "Did Lizzie not bar you?"

"No!" Kenna's eyes swivelled to the bar itself but the crowd was such that the personnel behind it were hidden from view. That worked both ways. Loney tried not to smile. "To continue, Reverend Loney, the great man – in his own eyes – is at this moment being questioned regarding a previous attempt on Jackie's life, to which deplorable action, he has admitted." For a second or two, Loney was stunned. Was she just talking nonsense? But Loney knew Kenna of old.

"You know, Kenna, you should never have given up on that law degree all those years ago," said Loney smiling.

"They were all a bunch of.."

"Now, now, Ms Duguid, Loney as was, once upon a time." Kenna ignored him.

"Now, let's leave the has-beens alone – for good," she said, "and discuss this McChesney business for I've a nice bit of info for you." Kenna was savouring the results of her telling blow as she pretended to being unable to locate the letter in her bag.

"Forget the McChesneys!" said Loney more decisively than he felt.

"Oh no, Gary, there's something in this that is more intriguing than your scumbag brother's future welfare. What's the worst that could befall him? No capital punishment these enlightened days and no worrying where the rent's coming from. Could be better than

being the heir. He's sorted. You see, I do have a very caring side. Now, I've had a long talk with Auld Dan and his telling words were, 'You should have asked Jackie. Pity about the dementia. He could maybe have told you all about it.' Now, Gary, I don't give a tinker's damn who wrote those letters. That person's bit is over and done with, ours isn't. So, the next step?" Kenna waited. Loney had never been one to resist a challenge. But he shook his head slightly.
"Too busy, too much to think about. You're on your own." Kenna slammed her notebook into her bag again.
"As always. Well, have it your own way. Be seeing you. My ma's bringing Jojohn back for Rhys's funeral. The Duguids are coming with them for a bit of a break and a lot of shopping. The 'flu has taken a lot out of them and they're now ready to hit the town in a rather weakened sort of way. The Barras, probably. Could you put Jojohn up?"
"Of course, anytime, you know that." Kenna looked oddly hesitant.
"I've told nobody about the will," she said quietly – for Kenna.
"Principally because you shouldn't have read it in the first place, I presume?" said Loney frowning.
"Principally because that self-styled legal eagle of an ex-husband wants to spring it on the police as a sort of coup d'etat. No motive for killing his da. Pretend he knew about it all the time. But that was actually before the other matter of attempted murder arose. Absolutely nothing to do with me."

The Ginger Bottle

"He's got the will at the police station?" asked Loney. Kenna smiled a rare smile and, Loney thought, it was a most becoming one. He had to admit that with all her very obvious faults, she was a much more intriguing woman than Summer.

"Not at this precise moment, he hasn't. He dropped it as he left the church hall. Put it in his inside pocket. Clapped out like its owner and the will fell right through the hole."

"And you very kindly picked it up," suggested Loney. Kenna nodded.

"Safe and sound. I'll provide the lawyers' names when asked. After all, this is just a copy. But, dear ex-brother-in-law, as you have signed off the true mystery round here, I shall go it alone. I found out at a very early age to rely on nobody. I will not, as they say, keep you posted." Loney knew that that lack of trust had defined Kenna's entire life and he felt immensely sorry and guilty about it. She viewed it like that and everyone else saw her as an extremely selfish person. Maybe, just maybe, something had pushed an extremely self-centred child into be what amounted to, more or less, a loner.

Somebody took his plate and mug away. Loney was too wrapped up in his thoughts and personal grief for his father to notice. He made a determined effort to pull himself together as Malky Vipond bore down on him through the throng.

"This place is going like a fair. That Lizzie Loudon must be worth a fortune."

"It's the pies," said Loney smiling as Vipond took the chair so recently vacated by Kenna. The Ginger

The Ginger Bottle

Bottle was famous for its beer. As an old coaching inn, it had once boasted a restaurant as well and its reputation had been second only to the Tontine and the Saracen's Head in the old days.

"I think the world's gone crazy, Gary." Vipond looked round for a waiter.

"It was always teetering on the brink, Malky. Glad you could make it." Vipond placed his laptop on the settle beside Loney.

"I've been hearing a few rumours regarding Robert." Loney wondered if this was to be the main topic of conversation, not young Rhys's tragic end, not even Jackie Loney – a man who had spent his entire life within the streets surrounding The Ginger Bottle where he had died a violent death – but on the man who was helping the police with their investigations. Loney wondered how many had decided that his elder brother had killed his father and how many had firmly denied that he was capable of it. A majority would simply sit on the fence or maybe just agree with whoever they were talking to.

"What's being said, Malky?" They both waited until the requested large sausage roll and coffee were placed before the monumental sculptor and he had savoured the first bite.

"I phoned ahead. Lizzie's my wife's cousin," Vipond explained and liberally treated the coffee to sugar. He bit off another piece and Loney watched him chew, thoughtfully. The sourdough had now had its day. "As I said, rumour-mill employees working overtime. I'll list them, the rumours that is, and you can choose the order of merit, Gary. This sausage roll is seriously good, by the way."

"It looks it," replied Loney with feeling. Vipond took the hint, cut off a piece reluctantly from the untouched end and Loney felt a soothing sensation run the entire length of his lean body. "So, Malky, these rumours, what is the person on the street, and probably also in here, saying?"

"Rumours aplenty, but if you insist, I'll give you a few. First though, you'll have to accept that although you and I think that Robert has always been a whingeing loudmouth – now Robert and Kenna were surely a match made in Hell – and nothing more, the general populace has not been so partisan or generous in its estimation of your brother." Loney agreed and it showed.

"So, the general opinion as to Robert being capable of murder is, in fact, that he is. Am I right?" suggested Loney.

"More than capable." Vipond refilled his cup from the small coffee-pot as he spoke. Loney did not even attempt to hide his surprise.

"I can't accept that, Malky."

"Which bit? That he is capable of that or that generally folk think that he is?"

"Both."

"Nobody's asking you to. I'm simply telling you what's being said by folks who've known him all his life, folk who know how desperate he is for money, folks who know that he threatened to kill your da. Now, you and I are of the same mind, Gary. Robert's harmless but he's always been very volatile. Put him under extreme pressure and who knows what he might do."

"But he isn't under extreme pressure. He'd have come to me if he needed help," Loney protested but knew he might just be talking tripe. He himself had been on the receiving end of Robert's violent temper many times when they were younger.

"Okay, we'll leave it at that just for a moment and look at the other rumours. They'll maybe give you food for thought. Our book-keeper's always on about cumulative totals. In other words, maybe there were just too many wee problems and in a moment of volcanic pressure, they all reached his consciousness at the same time and Robert's temper erupted in a devastating, Krakatoa fashion."

"I'm listening," said Loney quietly.

"All these rumours seem to have their roots in conversations of a very fraught kind taking place between your da and your brother when the kitchen window was wide open or when the pair of them were on the landing. They were both well-liked so there's no settling old scores here. Jackie Loney was always known as a gentleman, always willing to help his neighbours and Robert was always just a daft boy who never quite grew up. Probably the women just felt sorry for him having been married to Kenna, Ivan the Terrible's sound-alike."

"Alright," said Loney, "what exactly did they see and hear that changed their attitude to Robert so dramatically?"

"Seems it was his more recent behaviour and you da's, too, since the dementia clouded his thinking a bit now and then. Your da was his usual affable self unless frustration took over and his reaction to being thwarted could be a bit aggressive. All talk and no action, it seems, but if the person on the receiving end was himself depressed, well, we're all human." This was all new territory to Loney and he was loath to reveal that he had never seen any of this. Had he neglected his own family, he wondered guiltily, when they had needed him most? Vipond continued relentlessly. "The first major incident between them seems to have been about your mother's jewellery."

"There was only a ring or two and a few earrings. That was about it, Malky." Maybe more than a few, he suddenly thought, for his mother's family had been well-off and she had inherited a small but fine collection from her own mother. Loney had forgotten all about the jewellery. "What had it to do with Robert?" he asked suddenly.

"He'd taken the lot. Pawned them without your da's permission. Jackie was seen chasing Robert out the door with a toffee hammer before two plumbers from Parkes and Stadles at Bridgeton Cross managed to take it from him. They thought it was a bit of a laugh but stressed-out Robert collapsed in a heap and had to be helped downstairs and into one of the bottom flats for a strong cup of tea and an empire biscuit. Rumour has it that it was all so traumatic for him, he required two empire biscuits before recovery set it. Your da just sat back down to watch the telly as if nothing had happened. All done, yesterday's news."

"And the next bit of gossip?" asked Loney sourly.

"The shoe was on the other foot this time. There's a bench or common grass are just under your da's kitchen window." Loney nodded. "One fine day, some old biddies were passing the time there reminiscing when raised voices cut it short. Verbal battles over money are not remotely interesting but, over a gold watch, well that's something new."

"The half-hunter?" asked Loney resigned to hearing the worst. Vipond nodded

"That's it. Now why Robert would want it is anybody's guess."

"Pawnshop fodder," said Loney. Both men ignored the constant ringing of their mobiles. "It was my Granda's watch. It hung from his waistcoat on a very heavy gold chain."

"Are the two still together?" asked Vipond. Loney thought for a moment.

"I haven't seen them in years but they were when I last did. Do you think Robert would try to take that, too?" Vipond was forced to answer in the affirmative. "Probably, but it seems your da was having one of his better days. When Robert accused him of with-holding his inheritance from him, Jackie told him to bugger-off. Robert yelled that he'd beat the whereabouts of the hiding-place out of him and the sound of smashing crockery and screams emanating from Jackie's flat bore witness to the fact that Robert was being as good as his word. A couple of young hoodie types passing by scaled the drainpipe and went in through the window. Everyone else headed for the stairs. Robert was sitting on top of Jackie and in the act of bringing a stool down on his da's face.

One of the boys yanked him up just in time and decided to chuck him out of the window. One of the neighbours yelled at them to stop as he might hit her washing, so they settled for giving Robert a bit of a superficial thumping and then they took Jackie for a pint here in The Ginger Bottle."

"Seems like the Young Glasgow Hero of the Year award will be earned courtesy of various incidents up the same close," remarked Loney.

"Involving the same people?" asked Vipond.

"More or less."

"Anyway, keep your eyes open for the watch and chain when you're clearing the flat, Gary." Vipond finally finished off the sausage roll and coffee.

"Well, the Loneys have certainly given the locals plenty to talk about, Malky."

"There are other lesser quarrels but those are the main two. Actually the main piece is that last one I've just mentioned. It's regarded as the final act of desperation and fear for Robert's own life. The basic motive was that simply because it seems to be well-known among the gambling fraternity hereabouts that Robert is heavily in debt due to online gambling. If his father was refusing to throw what was a final lifeline, it's conceivable that Robert's volatile nature would come to the fore knowing that his situation was then helpless. That would put him at the mercy of debt enforcers of the worst possible kind." There was along pause and Vipond signalled to the barmaid for more coffee, decaff this time, and two mugs. The coffee and mugs duly arrived, Vipond poured and both men helped themselves to milk and sugar.

The Ginger Bottle

"Still doesn't make him guilty, Malky," said Loney, thoughtfully stirring his coffee.

"My thoughts exactly, Gary, for as I said a while back, I don't believe he did it. I think that having heard about that stool business, he would be capable under these very trying circumstances, but also that he would not have the composure or nerve to deny it. Robert's more the non-stop confessing type." Loney looked at Malky Vipond. Malky's brother Murdy had been the same age as Jackie Loney but Malky was a good bit younger. Malky stirred his coffee with deep deliberation.

"There's something else, isn't there?" said Loney. The monumental sculptor seemed to come to a difficult decision and raised his eyes to Loney's.

"You're not going to like this, Gary," he warned. But Loney just waited and stroked Fat Face who had climbed onto his knee and was eyeing Vipond's laptop with deep suspicion.

"Let's have it," said Loney, "I've got my comfort blanket now." Fat Face purred with delight.

"Alright. Robert was really desperate. He'd tried to kill himself in the old graveyard, Old Calton. A rope and a sturdy branch, only he didn't pick one sturdy enough. Your brother was at the end of his tether, Gary. Bella found him, took him into the bakery and sorted him out. I got that from Tina in the bakery."

"They were always very close, Bella and Robert," said Loney slowly. He felt a complete and utter failure. He decided to forget asking Malky about Norma and Leonard which was why Malky was in The Ginger Bottle. Loney had phoned him earlier on

The Ginger Bottle

that morning and had arranged to meet up in the pub. Things were bad enough and he suspected that Malky thought he had intended asking the latest talk about Robert.

"Mr Vipond, Malky, got a minute?" called a voice from the door as the woman then elbowed her way through Lizzie's patrons. "Knew where to find you as you said that you were seeing the Reverend Loney about another inscription on his mother's headstone in Janefield." Loney felt ashamed that he had used that as an excuse.

"I am. How was Lanzarote, Sharon?" asked Vipond.

"Rotten. Food indifferent. Glad I took a bag of shortbread. Next November's pre-Christmas trip will be in Inverness. A coach trip, fine hotel and no stag-parties allowed. Or hen nights either for that matter."

"I suppose you wanted a word with me, Sharon?" asked Vipond pointedly.

"That I do. I heard that you were wondering where that note came from, the one about the McChesney gravestone." Loney's interest perked up in spite of everything.

"I was. This is our cleaner, Mr Loney." Loney smiled at Sharon as she continued.

"I saw it being left on your desk. I nipped along when I saw somebody sneak into the office. I watched and saw him leave, made sure he didn't take anything. Couldn't figure it out. Well, anyway, I recognised the person. It was Rhys Ronaldson. He was at school with my son."

Chapter 6

Loney sat on the wall outside the London Road police station and waited for his brother's imminent release. The heavy fog was descending again and was making visibility poor and the air dank and brown. He was wearing a suit, black and woollen as matched his heavy coat, and he felt the better for the touch of luxury it gave him. He had spent a restless, sleepless night. Summer had turned as cold as winter and he could not be bothered humouring her before she drove back to her own flat by the river. Kenna and her brutish tongue. She was Jojohn's mother and Loney and Jojohn were very close. To keep his nephew in his life, he had to accept Kenna's occasional sorties into it as well. He glanced behind him. Plenty of comings and goings but no sign of Robert and his Legal Aid lawyer. No sign of Robert's latest girlfriend either. He was consumed with guilt over letting his own brother down.

"So, you've condescended to show your face, have you?" Loney's guilt vanished abruptly as he watched the lawyer scurry past him with an expression of relief and sympathy on his pale countenance. Loney suspected that he had worked hard for his money.

"You've convinced them of your innocence then, Robert?"

"Not quite. The old devil had phoned Bella's Bakery and told her to deliver a bacon roll and a buttered one ten minutes after I was spotted in St Mungo Street with Jimmy Turnbull. Bella told him to naff-off. I'm

suing that lot back in there for wrongful arrest and then I'll leave this benighted city for points west. Miami, probably, I think." Robert finally stopped talking.
"And sink holes. You were never arrested." Robert Loney ignored this remark.
"Where's the will? That copy's mine. It's part of da's estate and goes to the executor."
"Who's that?" asked Loney.
"I don't know," Robert Loney admitted but simply brushed the whole idea aside.
"Why do you want to see it?"
"I intend scrutinising the fine print," said Robert firmly. By trade, Robert Loney was a marine engineer. He wasn't short of intelligence, just fatally short on common-sense.
"If the big print says you get nothing, the fine one will probably say you get less than nothing. Da wanted you excluded for reasons best known to himself so, obviously, he'll have seen to it that that would be exactly what happened when he died. Now, come on and we'll eat."

Loney took a few reheats from the fridge.
"I'll make us something to eat," he said. "Have a seat at the coffee-table. You know where everything is." The microwave went to work. "Released without charge, I take it." Robert nodded vigorously. "Too right. As if I would kill my own father. I'll take them for every penny I can get from their budget. Or somebody's budget, anyway."
"You admitted one attempt to kill Da," said Loney, eyeing the microwave.

"There's a big difference between a half-hearted attempt in the throes of depression and actual murder."
"You're right there, Robert, two neds to be exact."
Robert shifted uncomfortably.
"I was depressed."
"And the suicide attempt?" Loney's brother just shrugged.
"Aw, that was just an act to get Jimmy Turnbull to take me with him to a concert that night. Knew his wife would fall for it and persuade him. I'd heard his pal had pulled out."
"You're a waste of space, Robert. You can't even be honest with yourself." The microwave pinged and Loney slammed the casserole reheats onto the kitchen table and pointed to one of the cupboards. Robert took the hint and finally got out the plates and cutlery. They ate in silence for a while.
"I'm thinking of contesting that will," Robert said finally. Loney was rapidly becoming exasperated.
"For goodness sake, the sole heir is your own son."
"That's what you think!" Robert kept his eyes firmly on the sausage and chilli casserole in front of him. Suddenly he pushed it away and stood up. "Think I'll buy a macaroni pie downstairs," he said.
"That requires money. Now finish what's in front of you and explain that last comment." But Robert was regretting his outburst.
"I don't mind halving the lot with the boy." Loney sighed deeply.
"Talk sense. Da deliberately excluded you in favour of Jojohn."

The Ginger Bottle

"He excluded me by mistake. He really meant you. When he attacked me, he thought I was you, thought I'd done him down all these years when it was really you."

"You've some imagination, I'll grant you that," said Loney, looking ruefully at the chilli.

"I've witnesses. He hit me with his stick in the street calling me Gary at one point. He was shouting that you'd cheated him. That was what was on his mind when he wrote that will. He wasn't in his right mind."

Loney suddenly found himself laughing.

"He was when he wrote it for it was dated a week after Jojohn was born, nineteen years ago, long before dementia had even begun."

"You were the one who should've been given the punt."

"Be happy for your son for Da could have left the lot to the Canine Defence League. He loved Fat Face better than any human bar Ma he'd ever met."

Robert was thinking out his alternatives.

"Maybe I'll have a word with Jojohn. When is he due back?" he asked abruptly.

"Some time today and once Josie hears about the will, she'll treat you like a leper and your chances of leaning hard on the boy will be zero. Are you finished eating?"

"Only one course? Was that it? You're a miserable swine."

"There's always the macaroni pie in the fridge," Loney suggested gathering up the plates.

"You should check the use-by date. Besides, I can't stand Italian grub."

"I doubt if there's an Italian alive who would claim it as an authentic dish." Loney made a mental note to check all the use-by dates for it had been a few weeks since he had done so.

"Be seeing you. Thanks for nothing." With that Robert Loney exited down the outside staircase, not the inside one, and headed for God only knew where.

Loney made himself a mug of tea and decided it was time to try and pull it all together. He had to make sure Jojohn did not fall for his father's pleas for money. Suddenly, he decided that enough was enough. To hell with the McChesney letters. He had enough on his plate without chasing will-o-the-wisps. He now felt that a load had been lifted from his mind. But a text right then put it all back into his court. The final arrangements for Rhys Ronaldson's funeral. Had the boy's death really been an accident? Why had he called for Loney to watch out? Why had he left that packet on Malky Vipond's desk and who had put him up to it? Jojohn was due within a few hours, he thought. Those two had been inseparable. Perhaps Rhys had confided in him.

He welcomed the calm that came with occupying once more his seat by the crackling hearth in the bar of The Ginger Bottle.

"This pub's haunted."

"By a satisfied or disappointed customer, Dan?"

"A former landlord. Waiting still for Bonnie Prince Charlie and his mates to settle their bill."

"He'll have some wait then. But what brought that fine gentleman to mind, Dan? The landlord, I mean," asked Loney.

The Ginger Bottle

"Association, and it wasn't Prince Charles Edward Stuart who has made the big impression on me but the landlord." Loney laid aside his newspaper.

"Go ahead, Dan, I'm listening."

"I'm a direct descendant, you know." Loney had just had the worst two days of his life but he found himself grinning like a Cheshire cat. Fat Face dug its claws into Loney's legs as it sprang onto his knees. Loney's expression changed.

"Yes, I can see that. All you need is the wig and the dozy expression." Dan suffered almost in silence.

"The King across the Water was even more skint than I am for I suppose that's who you are referring to." Dan shook his head slowly at the Man of the Cloth's ignorance. "All this," and here his skinny arm etched a wide sweep of the crowded bar, "all this," he repeated, "should be mine." Loney nodded and accepted the rebuke.

"I stand corrected, sir."

"The landlord, the Ghost of Christmas Past, was my 4 or 5 times great grandfather no less, and I'll thank you, Mr Loney, to remember that I am a republican."

"As well as a frustrated publican, Dan?"

"Quite so."

"And the point of all this is what?"

"The point is that the history of this area, well, Abercromby Street and environs anyway, has taken place with my family's business at its hub."

"And when did it stop being owned by your illustrious forebears?" asked Loney thoroughly enjoying himself.

The Ginger Bottle

"When the ghost of Jeremiah McNab first put in an appearance. You see, minister, he'd left it to his daughter, the fair Grizel, and she got shot of it pronto to her cousin; vanished with her fancy man, spent the lot on partying big style in London and then just dropped dead at the horse-racing."

"I take it that that is the first point, Dan, so what's the second?" asked Loney.

"The second and final point is that my ancestors were not renowned for their sagacity. In other words, they were all as thick as mince. The next owner died within one year of inheriting having overdosed on his own product, food not booze. So, it looks like Jeremiah showed no sense at all in leaving a goldmine he'd taken a lifetime to build up to a flibberty-gib of a daughter. The next heir sold the lot as soon as he'd got it to a complete stranger and hopped it for South Australia where he was reputed to have been the main course on somebody's Sunday lunch in a remote island when he was shipwrecked en route. Seems that I've inherited that cavalier spirit."

"Only you're a republican."

"Right. Now I'm here to try and help you find a way out of the maze that concerns these letters. I'm doing so, not that I see a hope in hell of succeeding, because one bit of info, useless or otherwise, will help ease my somewhat refined conscience. You see, minister, I've a big mouth and I think that this time my throwaway indiscretion might just have caused a fatality. I'll have a pint of my usual, Lizzie!" Dan roared across the hubbub knowing that Loney's nod meant that he'd be paying as usual. Pity, he thought,

The Ginger Bottle

that Loney was a strict traditionalist in some respects. The Ginger Bottle had the minister's total loyalty and Dan knew that his much longed for chance of experimenting with the in-favour cocktails in the new wine-bar was non-existent. Loney waited patiently and signalled for a teapot refill. "I think I might have killed your da, son." The barmaid placed Dan's pint before him and then took Looney's teacup away from him. The saucer remained on the table. He suddenly fancied some buttered toast, signalled to Lizzie and thought that he should perhaps buy a very small but efficient pencil sharpener. He broke off the wood that now shielded the lead of his Ikea pencil and then smiled at Dan.

"Dan, last week you thought you'd killed Kennedy."

"A careless word, that's all it takes, Gary, and I've let slip a few very careless ones in my day. It can inspire or, I should perhaps say, incite people's murderous thoughts." Dan sniffed short and drank long.

"And the latest careless word concerning my da was?" Loney waited and tried not to laugh. Sometimes it seemed to him that a minister's work was split between drinking tea and trying not to laugh.

"Norma McChesney. Two words, actually." Loney was now intrigued.

"So, exactly what did you say, for I assume it was words and not doing the actual murder?" Dan nodded decisively.

"Yes. Gary, I brought up the subject while your da and I were just sitting in his flat talking about the old days. I think your da felt more comfortable in the

The Ginger Bottle

past these days and, frankly, I don't care much for the present myself."

"So, you were both strolling down memory lane when you arrived at the close all of you stayed up," Loney suggested.

"Right. That actually came about because Jackie had found a box of old photos and we were going through them. There was one with a lot of young folk going into a wedding reception. It was just a group of guys. I spotted Leonard Wylie and that brought Norma McChesney back to mind."

"Why was that?"

"I'd heard the McChesney name mentioned some days before."

"You mean someone was talking about that family before you'd heard about the letters?"

"Must have been, can't remember who, though. I have a wide circle of acquaintances, you understand, and I might just have overheard a part of somebody else's conversation," Dan explained patiently.

"I do understand," said Loney. Dan was a fixture in the social life of an area still inhabited by families such as Dan's who had lived there for generations. Loney knew that there were still small areas of the city that had managed to evade the catastrophic history-cleansing blitz of the city's councillors.

"What did you say to my da, Dan?"

"Well, I knew better than to mention Norma McChesney's name for she'd been the great love of your da's life. You see, son, as a man gets older and retreats into the past, all the great times fade and the memory sort of time-jumps back to that first love, invests it with a value it never really had."

"Reality finally kicks in but not with my da. Dementia was taking over," said Loney sadly.

"I'm afraid so, Gary. I kind of took your da back to what was probably one of the darkest episodes of his life for he was always a romantic fool. Sorry, spoke out of turn there, sorry. He got very fired up about it, started pointing and swearing at Leonard Wylie in the photo. I managed to calm him down in the end. When the elopers left, Jackie had really set out to blacken Leonard's character. He made all sorts of ridiculous accusations concerning other girls – you know, hints at rape and assaults, that kind of thing. Just as well everybody took it with a pinch of salt and that Norma and Leonard were on the other side of the Atlantic. I expect that having no Facebook and Twitter helped. Here's your toast." Loney bit into a half-slice. "Ever tried putting a square-sliced sausage on that, Gary?" Loney nodded, Dan savoured his pint.

"Frequently," said Loney and smiled. He knew that his wholesome diet would finally rid him of the delectable Summer McNaughten. He glanced at Fat Face's receding form and knew that butter was not to that feline's taste. "Leonard Wylie, Dan, tell me about him." Maybe this was all just Wylie strolling down memory lane, too. Had he come back home, noted the inscription and wondered what it was all about? Was it giving him some belated revenge on the man who had so bad-mouthed him in the past to use that man's son to stir up old memories and rake up Jackie's verbally, violent past?

"Leonard Wylie was all mouth, got the patter. He was a car salesman when ordinary people were just about earning enough to be almost able to afford one. He liked the girls and they certainly liked him. He always dressed to kill when the rest of us only did that on a date. We were all in the Parkhead Forge or in one of the other heavy engineering works. Any old combination of clothes was good enough for factory work or even at the docks. We were mostly apprentices, earning less than he was at that time, but with overtime, it gave us quite a healthy sum. But it really wasn't the money, it was the suits and the ties and the chat-lines that separated Leonard from the rest of us. Gary, your da was ranting about being a suspect in their murder case – one that never existed – and I suggested to him that he get you to clear his name." Loney was relieved that he now finally knew how he came to be implicated in his father's confused thoughts.

Lizzie Loudon suddenly appeared and sat down on the settle beside Loney. Dan decided that he would make himself scarce for Lizzie had that dismissive look on her face. She turned to Loney as Dan disappeared out the door.

"Jojohn's upstairs and waiting outside your flat, Gary. He doesn't look a great deal better, though," she said wryly.

Loney took the inside stairs three at a time despite his dicky knee. Josie was whispering, Jojohn nodding vigorously.

The Ginger Bottle

"Thanks, Granny. Hello, Uncle Gary. Granny here's trying to cheer me up. She's letting me take the lead in the style competition coming up in Birmingham in January. That's a really big showcase." Jojohn turned to Josie. "I won't let you down, Granny." Josie smiled.

"I always said you had the talent but now you have the motive. Keep your eye on your career and it'll take you through this very rough time, Jojohn." Gary let Jojohn and Josie into the flat.

"Did you ever hear Granda mentioning the name McChesney, Jojohn" asked Loney quietly as he and his nephew sat on the sofa. Jojohn sighed and fiddled with the remote TV control.

"During these last few months he was always muttering, talking to himself. No harm in that, though, I'd say. He liked to talk as if Granny Loney was just in the next room. Not all the time, though, just now and again really."

"And the name McChesney, ever heard him mention it?"

"Have you been asked to take a funeral, another person you know nothing about?" Gary asked. Loney smiled. Gary knew his job almost as well as he did. "I might have heard that name. Never really took much notice, just sort of automatically filtered out what I thought might be relevant to today. I loved my Granda, Uncle Gary, and he loved me. He was always good to me. I bought this suit in Perth for his funeral with my own money. Rhys would have had a good laugh if he thought it was for his funeral. No hoodie. Granny here says it'll do for

The Ginger Bottle

both. Very respectful, she says." Loney obviously agreed.

"Was Granda ever a bit aggressive towards you, Jojohn?" Loney did not know what kind of an answer to expect but he had to ask.

"My granda never laid a finger on me, not once in all my life." Loney realised that Jojohn was evading his question on the McChesneys and he also knew how to get around it.

"But he was threatening to kill me, wasn't he?" Jojohn suddenly jumped up and slumped against the wall by the door.

"I was scared, Uncle Gary, scared to death. I needed help so that was why I wrote the letters."

Chapter 7

Loney was stunned into shocked silence.
"Which letters?" Josie looked quickly from her grandson to Loney. "Am I missing something here? Did you write that letter to your mother?" she asked tersely.
"Sit down both of you," said Loney. Even with just three adults, his sitting-room seemed crowded. Loney was slowly recovering from the shock. "Tell me all about it," he said quietly to Jojohn. The boy glanced at the disapproving look he was getting from Josie who had already decided that this was probably bad news. She did not take the hint from Loney to retire from the scene and let him do the talking. Jojohn decided his best way forward was to act as if his Granny Duguid had left.
"I sent you two letters, really notes I suppose, and one to Mum. It was all because Granda was acting funny, Granny, and I was dead scared." Josie shook her head before speaking.
"I told you that you were coming back here far too soon. Your pal Rhys was a very understanding lad. He would have been saying the same as would his folks. I had a phone-call from them last night and they were very keen that you should stay in Perth for a while for coming back here was not in your best interests. They're very fond of you, Jojohn." Josie stood up and looked over at Loney. "He's always been one for scribbling letters. He kept a diary faithfully for years until one day wee Natasha, next door's wean, got hold of it and scribbled and tore

The Ginger Bottle

most of it to bits. Well, I'm off. As he's staying here tonight, you can make a boys' night of it. I'll be in touch!" Loney saw Josie out.

"Tell me about the letters, Jojohn," said Loney sitting back down on the decrepit sofa. He really needed to get Lizzie to change it. "What exactly was it that Granda was doing that frightened you so much? Something to do with the McChesneys, was it?" Jojohn nodded.

"That's right. He was working himself up into a real frenzy one day and that's when I decided to ask for your help – in a roundabout sort of way."

"You could have just come to me, Jojohn, and I would have had a word with him."

"But that was the last thing I wanted. Actually, Uncle Gary, I don't really know what I wanted."

"Why's that?" Gary was leaning forward in the sofa now, his elbows resting on his knees, his hands supporting his chin. His hair was still immaculate. "Gary, son, start at the beginning and just let it flow." The boy nodded and thought for a bit.

"I remember what you once wrote in a book you gave me. It was a biography of Nelson Mandela and on the fly-leaf you had written, 'Let justice roll down like a stream of water and honesty like a flowing tide." I promised myself there and then that I would try to live that but, with the situation with Granda, my courage failed and I passed the buck on to you and Mum. I don't think they'll be naming any Glasgow squares after me." Loney laughed and a slight grin managed to shine through, for a very brief moment, the misery on Jojohn's young face.

The Ginger Bottle

"Go, I'm listening."

"I loved living with Granda whenever I could. He was funny and kind and caring. He could cook, too. He would turn up at all the school parents' evenings when nobody else would. Granny was always doing the late opening shift on a Thursday at Killer Kuts and the parents' meetings were either in the afternoon or a Thursday evening. But lately, well, Granda's been very confused but he always managed to get by and staying with him was still great."

"So, when and why did all this change?" Jojohn thought hardly at all as it was all too stark right then.

"About a month or so ago. I've no idea why but I know Auld Dan was involved. Somebody he'd met, something he might have just passed onto Granda. When I'd come back from the shop, I'd hear him muttering and throwing things about. Changed right away, back to his usual self, when he realised I was in the flat. Mind if I get myself a drink of water?" Loney shook his head and the moment his nephew was out of the room, he switched his mobile on and sent a text message to Lizzie. By the time Jojohn had followed up his drink with a visit to the toilet, Loney had received the answer to his request. There was no good reason that he could see for enlightening his nephew. It was all beginning to come together in Loney's mind but there were still huge gaps and no name in the frame for his father's killer.

"Feel like continuing?" Jojohn sat back down and seemed eager to talk.

The Ginger Bottle

"Oh yes, for it's helping to set it all out straight and simple and it's telling me how to understand that change in Granda."

"Good. Soon as you like then." Loney sat back and waited.

"They began to become more frequent, these outbursts. The mutterings stopped and he began talking very loudly and threatening somebody. Whenever I asked if he'd like to tell me about it, about who was really annoying him, who had made him so angry and why, he'd just clam up and go to his bed no matter what the time was." Jojohn was now retreating into the recent past and Loney knew that at the most, he should simply have to prod him a little.

"And the McChesneys? Did he mention them, Jojohn?"

"Just one of them. It was a girl or woman called Norma. Quite a nice name really, isn't it?" Jojohn seemed to dwell on it a little then suddenly came alive again. "Anyway, at first, I thought it was a family he knew or had known and that she'd done something to upset him but he was also talking about a Ford Cortina. Now, as you know, mechanical things hold no interest for me, Uncle Gary, so I just mentioned the name to Rhys and he said it was built in the 1960s or thereabouts. Granda was obviously reliving the past but wasn't aware of it. He seemed to be blaming the car for something. Does all this make any sense to you? Any impression at all?" Loney smiled to uplift the tension in the small room.

"It would if it was driven over me, I suppose. Jojohn, I think that your granda was implying that the manufactured qualities of that Cortina had trumped his own more natural ones." Gary twigged straight off.
"I see, a guy with a flash car beat him to it in the romance stakes then, eh?"
"That about sums it up." Both of them grinned at the thought.
"I told Rhys about a family named McChesney who had upset Granda and he said he'd ask around. Rhys is – was, much in demand so it took him a while to come back with the answer. Seems he couldn't track down anybody with that name. Granda was getting more and more worked up and I had just sat back and waited, wasted, nearly a week for Rhys to finish his enquiries. So, I just took the bull by the horns and asked you and Mum because Granda had begun threatening to kill you, Uncle Gary, for spreading rumours about him. He actually rammed the kettle into the bin because it was taking too long to boil. The kettle and water were suddenly no more."
"Why didn't you tell me, Jojohn?" Why was Loney putting the guilt on his nephew? He felt ashamed but Jojohn was answering before he could retract that question and apologise.
"Who wants to be told somebody wants to kill him? But, if I'm honest, it wasn't only that. He'd begun to get annoyed with me, too, and I was scared stiff. So, I wrote the letters. Well, actually, I typed them on the computer. Sort of faked a signature."

"A warning and a plea for help at the same time." Jojohn nodded miserably.

"And now I hear that folks are saying my da topped him."

"Do you think he's capable of doing that?" asked Loney watching Jojohn closely. The boy shrugged.

"He's just a wind-bag and a layabout, but he's got a violent temper and I've never heard him say a kind word to Granda. But when I think about it all seriously, I've never heard him say a kind word to anybody. All things considered, probably not. He's a waste of space whose got a big mouth and nothing to back it up. In short, Uncle Gary, he's a coward."

"I got the second note by hand from a mysterious person. Who delivered it as I nearly froze to death waiting outside the Old Calton Burial Graveyard?" asked Loney.

"I know. I saw the cargo pants and the sweatshirt." Jojohn smiled broadly. "I expect you've guessed." Loney nodded. "Rhys offered to do it when he saw the weather forecast on TV. He said it would add a bit of mystery when he loomed out of the fog like that. He suggested making it as early as possible so that along with the heavy fog, it would still be dark. As Granda liked to make my breakfast for me when I stayed overnight, it wasn't early at all for there was no way I was going to put his usual routine out. Also, I had only given Rhys a very short outline of what was going on and, as his eyesight left a lot to be desired and with the darkness, he'd have had no chance to study the note between getting it from me at the last minute and meeting you by the cemetery

The Ginger Bottle

gates. He just thought it was all a bit of a joke anyway. It was about you and Granda and that was private. Even Rhys wasn't to know and he understood that. Anyway, Rhys wasn't nosey. He'd delivered that letter about the headstone inscription and the money to Mr Vipond's office without asking for any details."

"Then that was why you felt so guilty, he wouldn't have been there but for you? Is that it?" asked Loney. But Jojohn shook his head emphatically.

"No, Uncle Gary, he would have been there for he always hung about there. But I wouldn't have been there and so he wouldn't have finished up under that bus. I'd realised I hadn't posted a letter, a bill, and I ran down to the pillar-box by the lights at the foot of the street. I was just hurrying back when it all kicked off. The letters to you had taken up so much of my time thinking about them that I'd forgotten all about paying the bill. Rhys quite often went for Auld Dan's newspaper but I couldn't have said for certain that the guy outside The Ginger Bottle was Dan. I didn't think you wanted guesswork. You don't usually." Loney smiled.

"Think you could manage a quick flick over my head with the scissors, Jojohn?" he asked. It was about the only thing he could think of right then to take the boy's mind off Rhys's death.

"Got the gear in that case there and it's on the house," said Jojohn and he rose quickly. He was as eager to switch his thoughts as far away from that incident as he possibly could.

The Ginger Bottle

Loney had left the boy watching the telly. He felt that a few more things had now been eliminated and an equally few illuminated. He entered The Ginger Bottle lounge-bar but this time slipped behind the bar and knocked on the door marked 'Office'. He entered at Kenna's challenging 'Come in!" Loney did so.

"I'm watching the shop," she explained with a grin," for Lizzie's just slipped out. Cosy, isn't it? We're pals again." That was nothing new, thought Loney.

"Certainly looks cosy," answered Loney.

"She left this letter for you," said Kenna passing him the sealed envelope across the desk. She watched closely as Loney read the contents. "Care to share?"

"Only with a fish supper." But Loney sat down anyway in Lizzie's chair behind the desk thus signalling the joint effort had begun. He glanced at the note and then slipped it into his pocket. "Ladies first. I know the French for that," he said languidly, elbows on the desk.

"And I know how you came to know it and a good few other French phrases as well, Reverend Loney. But your secret is safe with me."

"No secret," he said, "evening leisure classes."

"I heard that it was more of hands-on that heads-down."

"Not at the price I was paying and me a most impoverished student, it wasn't. Had a hankering at the time for a spell at The Scots Kirk in Paris. Now, let's get to the point." Loney looked Kenna straight in the eye, hoped she wouldn't delve any deeper and waited. She was not easily intimidated so he knew that it suited her to talk.

"You always had a way with words. I just can't understand why that Norwegian beauty dumped you." Kenna was reluctant to give up savouring the moment.

"Neither can I!" They both laughed and then Kenna removed her A4 notebook from her latest 'suitcase' bag. Loney prepared to jot down a few notes on the back of Lizzie's sticky-notes pad. He wondered if his Ipad was still behind the bar.

"I take it, Gary, that we both think that there's a connection between these letters and your da's murder?" Kenna asked.

"Yes." Loney did not waste time asking how she had reached that conclusion.

"I take it you've been talking to your mother?" Kenna nodded.

"I just dropped in to ask her how the boy was doing. She's sorting out appointments in Killer Kuts."

"So where do we go from here, Kenna?" asked Loney watching her closely. She was clever and quick-thinking and it did not do to underestimate her. She jumped on his question.

"You know fine where we go. That note someone left for you just now."

"Could be someone from my congregation. They do have first call on my services, you know," he said sarcastically.

"Text you, call in the lounge-bar here, knock on your outside door. Those stairs need cleaning, by the way. That's how it's usually done, Reverend Loney."

The Ginger Bottle

Loney took the notepaper from its envelope, glanced at it once more, and then passed it over to Kenna.
"Is this it?" she asked tightly.
"You gave it to me, dear," he answered grinning.
"Question 1. It says or asks, I should say, who was Auld Dan talking to a month ago?" Kenna looked across at Loney. "Who the hell is Justin Cronin? Or is that Justine?" she asked peering at Lizzie's writing.
"No idea but I'm sure you can find out." He sat on in silence and Kenna took up the challenge. At last some sort of recognition seemed to filter through her thoughts.
"There was a Dr Cronin along at Broad Street. Not in my day. But he'd be long dead by now so what could be the connection?" she asked puzzled by this new name now in the frame.
"The McChesneys had lived there once upon a time. Kenna, think the Old Calton Burial Ground, the gravestones." But Kenna shook her head.
"Haven't had time to go there yet. Well, once almost but not quite. Got a phone-call. Did you see one there?" she asked. Loney nodded. "This all tells us absolutely nothing," Kenna protested. "Wait a minute. One of Dr Cronin's colleagues was a young Dr Wylie, a lady doctor as they used to say in the old days. Maybe the connection was Wylie, the irresistible gigolo. Could that meeting with Dan have been perfectly innocent?"
"Probably," Loney agreed, "but with dire consequences. What we really need to know is if Dan told my da all about this meeting, why did it all end in Da's death? Who could possibly have a

motive this far removed from that business so long ago for killing him? What could anybody have to gain?"

"Just simply settling an old score that had been festering for a lifetime," said Kenna thoughtfully.

"A doctor and a car salesman in those days was maybe a romantic bridge too far even if Dr Wylie was a cousin, so a scorned love is out. The next question is where was Wylie supposed to be that day?" said Loney doodling on the envelope. Victory was written all over Kenna Duguid's face as she spoke now.

"And the answer to that is Glasgow, fulfilling his last day at work. I haven't been hanging around, you know. He worked for Riley and Co at St Georges Cross. Now where does that get us?" Kenna asked sceptically. Loney looked at the envelope again.

"I'm just wondering if Da had been off work that day all those years ago."

"And seeking revenge," Kenna suggested dryly.

"Hardly that, come to think of it, as nobody knew about the elopement!" Suddenly Lizzie barged in and put in her tuppence worth. "Fat Face is dead!" She burst into tears.

"No, he isn't," said Loney, slight exasperation tingeing his words, "for he's in my flat with Jojohn. I think the boy's found a tin of sardines for the cat." Lizzie kissed Loney passionately and got roughly the same response. Kenna was scrutinising her notes and saw nothing.

"Thank God for that," said Lizzie eventually, "Auld Dan's barred. He told me it had been hit by a car in

London Road." She leaned back out of the door and relayed her proclamation to the bar-staff in a voice that could split rock. Kenna left without saying anything.
"Lizzie?" Loney waited, Lizzie nodded and his whole body seemed to shift on its axis. He had deliberately sent his last question by text to Lizzie and now he knew the answer.

Chapter 8

Loney's mind was racing, something he had seen, something he had heard, something he already knew. But what? He searched the farthest and deepest corners of his mind and knew that the answers would come to the fore – eventually. But he also knew that there really was no hurry unless – unless what? He already knew the answer to that one now from Lizzie and it was utterly ridiculous. Only one other person thereabouts had private transport. One accident, two murders, three what? It all sounded like the Christmas carol the small, almost tuneful choir of his congregation were already rehearsing for the service of Nine Carols and Songs. One partridge in a pear tree, two turtle doves and three French hens. There had only been one murder but something deep in his subconscious said that was wrong. If he could only remember.

"Lizzie, you've lived round here all your life." Lizzie nodded in agreement and watched the newly-arrived Fat Face wrestle with a toy mouse.

"Forever, as have you – almost. Even sat beside you in primary school."

"Even came out above Kenna and me in all the exams. So then, tell me this, do you recall anyone of our parents' generation discussing the elopement of Norma McChesney and Leonard Wylie? It was a nine-day wonder so it won't surprise me if they didn't think it was worthwhile talking about." He sat back in her chair and waited. Lizzie gave it some thought while tossing the mouse to Fat Face. That cat knew which side his bread was buttered, so to speak, for he really had an aversion to butter.

"My folks were running this pub, Gary, so it was bound to be talked about. Still, I only remember snatches amongst the women much later on, of course. Leonard Wylie? Was that his name? I never knew that, just the girl's, Norma McChesney. I think it was the fact that she came from a show-biz family that made it all so memorable."

"I thought it was the circus?" said Loney.

"Same thing, more or less. Circus and music hall or variety, if I remember correctly. Just ran away together. Don't know why they didn't just get married here. Seems she was mousy in a way but very gorgeous with it and he was a very handsome man. I think I've got some photos about here," said Lizzie looking about her. "My inheritance of the good old days when my widowed ma married an old flame and went to live the good life in Blackpool, God help them. Those photos are here somewhere for it was my da who really kept them. Let me see." Lizzie opened a filing cabinet, a wooden one, and produced a shoebox full of snaps. "The metal cabinets are for business purposes only, just in case the wooden one takes the fancy of some travelling woodworm," she explained frowning at it closely. "I had to buy this to accommodate the lot. Da was a great one for the snaps, lifetime member of the Mile End and District Camera Club. But this box is about the right era, I think. Have a look anyway, Gary, while I check up on that new waiter cum barman cum absolute plonker." Lizzie left and Loney flicked through the pages of the very thick album plus loose photos. Lizzie returned ten minutes later.

"Wylie was a handsome guy right enough and Norma's natural hair-colouring was like spun gold. Early coloured one. A very good-looking couple indeed," said Loney showing Lizzie the photo in his hand.

"Just so. No wonder that guy could have had his pick," said Lizzie whistling.

"Was it all public transport in those days round here, Lizzie?" he asked her, slowly replacing the photo.

"Before we came along? What do you want to know that for?" Loney shrugged.

"I don't rightly know. Just trying to visualise the place when our folks were young. Do you remember hearing anything?"

"Are you insinuating that all girls were gossip-mongers?" Loney laughed.

"Only you, Lizzie. You were always at your mother's side. Do you remember hearing anything about it when the older women were reminiscing over a cup of tea?" Lizzie nodded.

"Just bits here and there. Just tales of Norma's secret boyfriend and your da."

"My da?"

"Didn't you know?" Lizzie laughed.

"Just a word or two of late."

"Not surprised hardly anybody remembered for he took a lot of stick over it, I was told. He was probably trying to compete with that lad Wylie. His car was top notch, him being in the car trade but all your da could manage was a clapped-out wreck, it seems. Had to be pushed down the hill outside before it had any chance of starting. A Morris Minor, I think it was. Been in the wars before he got it. It needed half-a-dozen of his mates to push it before came to life, then some of them jumped in and off they went." Loney smiled with relief for any chance of his father following the eloping pair and killing them was now out of the question.

"I didn't know anything about a car," he said. "Was anything ever said about the day they took off?" Lizzie lifted the cat into her arms, the toy mouse dangling from its mouth.

"Fat Face reeks of sardines," she said indulgently. "Now, the elopement was only spoken of occasionally, a nine-day wonder like you said. It was all regarded as a bit of humour really. Evidently someone saw Mr Wylie offering Norma a lift so to speak and that was that. Had probably given him her case the previous evening. She'd left her auntie a note saying he'd promised to marry her and that she'd be in touch. It seems he'd handed his resignation, did the required notice and that day he'd given in the car to his company in Glasgow as arranged after picking Norma up. That was what the police said anyway. That seemed to be that. Didn't even last the nine days once the note to Norma's auntie had been found. It had slipped down the back of the sideboard unread and a week later, the cat eventually dragged it out to play with. You'd have thought they'd have bought the cat a wee toy mouse, wouldn't you, Fat Face? Folk were and are entitled to run away – fancy Blackpool, Gary? No? Paris?

The Ginger Bottle

No? – if they feel like it, so the police called the whole thing off although it had been half-hearted enough anyway, it seems." Loney's mind now seemed to be wandering and Lizzie waited. Did everybody know about that French girl, he wondered, panicking slightly? He suddenly stood up.

"Must be going. Lizzie, thanks for everything." Lizzie Loudon smiled as he walked to the door. She wondered if he would ever really look at her but realised that time was well past.

"Sure," she said, "wee Mrs Singleton handed this in for you." Loney was surprised as he looked at it, a woollen scarf. He never wore a scarf but he took it anyway. "It was lying on the landing outside your father's flat yesterday morning. She thought it might be his."

"Thanks. Be seeing you, Lizzie." He wandered back upstairs and wondered how Josie's scarf had come to be on that landing that day.

Jojohn had gone. Loney put on his parka and stuffed the Burberry scarf into the deep, inside pocket before heading for Kenna's flat across the street. Kenna was in.

"I'm going out." He gently brushed past her as she spoke.

"Won't keep you a minute," he said turning towards her.

"If it's your da's murder, leave it to the police." He shook his head.

"Can't do that, Kenna."

The Ginger Bottle

"Now if it's about the elopement, I'm listening," she said but continued to put on her jacket and scarf. It was a flimsy one as always.

"It's about the murder."

"Then I'm off," she repeated.

"Wait a minute. Once this is settled, I'll talk the other matter over with you, give it my best shot." Loney felt bad about it but she would be too caught up emotionally with the new situation and likely to muck it all up. He had to keep going regardless of everything else now. "People are saying Robert did it for the money. They say he didn't know about there being a will. Now you and I know that he did, he just wasn't exactly sure what was in it. Da had told him he'd get nothing but he didn't believe him. He thought my father wasn't that kind of a man. Who did you tell about it so that we can get to them and square it up? Was it just Jojohn?" He fervently hoped that it wasn't. Kenna finished arranging her scarf before speaking.

"I sent a text to my ma about the will, just to give her a laugh. Jackie had once hinted to me that Robert was getting nothing. He didn't mention you at all, Gary. I just supposed you'd get the lot. I'd forgotten about it. Just did it to give her a laugh. Two days ago Robert had gone into Killer Kuts and demanded a free haircut for old times' sake, he said. Caused a fuss in front of her high-flying customers. She was furious. Then I sent her one about Jackie dying some time later. I told her to use her own judgment as to when to pass the news on to Jojohn. He was

extremely upset about Rhys and I thought the news about his granda would have put him over the edge."
"When did you send the second text?" asked Loney.
"Just after she'd left for Perth and they'd found the body. Does he know yet?"
"He does. Thanks, Kenna. Lizzie and I were just strolling down memory lane," he said quite innocently, he hoped. "She has inherited some old photos of the area. Bit of a laugh, really."
"She's always thumbing her way through them. A waste of time." She opened the flat door and they both exited the flat, Kenna slamming it to behind them.
"I expect his new-found wealth might allow Jojohn to branch out a bit. Maybe he'll go it alone, maybe start with one of those travelling shops," said Loney.
"You mean do homers?" Kenna was not a woman to appreciate the subtleties of the English language despite her sally into the law at university.
"I suppose that's what I mean. Maybe a few days with Killer Kuts and some on his own with selected clients," Loney suggested, knowing absolutely nothing about the subject. But Kenna was intrigued.
"Could even buy a salon, save a bit," she mused.
"And Josie could advise him," he said and waited.
"No dice. He's already been made a partner by my ma and she'd never advise him to do home jobs. A one-way ticket to a lifetime of care homes, she says. She's been there, done it. See you at Rhys's funeral. Bye!" Loney watched as she sauntered up Abercromby Street.

The Ginger Bottle

Loney took a deep breath and walked into Killer Kuts.

"Where's Josie?" he asked rather sharply. Why did he want to see her – or did he?

"She's just nipped out to buy some biscuits." The receptionist cum hairdresser smiled sweetly as she answered, running her eyes over his tall, lean form. "Want a haircut? I could do it for you in a few minutes," she offered.

"Just had it done, thank you." The heat inside the salon was beginning to make him sweat.

"Could make you an appointment," she suggested. Loney shook his head and backed out into the crisp air. He had to think quickly, had to get it all straight in his mind.

He was leaning against the wall and watched as the traffic pounded its way down Abercromby Street. The noise was ear-splitting but somehow his mind was now completely focused on what he ought to be doing – stopping Josie from killing her grandson. When had Josie made Jojohn a partner and why? Had it been after that text about the will? Did she really need to kill his father? Would Loney himself have been next on the list if Jackie had not thought to omit both his sons? Had she in fact killed before? All those questions were searing Loney's brain and there was only one way to find out the answers. She would not be long and Loney decided to wait where he was and intercept her. The door of the salon opened and closed quickly and one of the stylists looked up and down the street.

The Ginger Bottle

"Have you seen Josie, Mr Loney?" she asked. Loney just shook his head. The door opened and closed once more. Josie liked her business to run on time, so, where was she? He straightened up. Where was Jojohn? In Loney's own flat. He dodged the traffic, entered The Ginger Bottle and raced up the stairs to the flat. He listened at the door. All was silent. He searched in his pockets for the key and quietly entered. But all remained silent, no-one was about anywhere. Dishes were piled clean on the drying rack, the basin tilted and empty, the sink pristine. He quietly closed the door again behind him.

Loney entered the lounge-bar.

"Are you looking for me, Gary?" The voice rang out across the crowded room and Loney looked over and saw Josie waving at him from his own settle seat. He smiled and made his way through to her and Auld Dan.

"Doesn't really matter now, Josie," he said sitting opposite her.

"My receptionist texted me. I'd got to blethering in the dairy. Sorry."

"That's alright. You weren't to know. I was just wanting a word with Jojohn. Know where he might be?" Loney asked brightly. Josie shook her head slowly.

"I'm afraid my guess would be as good as yours, Gary. He did say that maybe he'd take a walk along the Clydeside just to clear his head, order his thoughts."

"When did he say that?"

The Ginger Bottle

"Just before I went into the dairy," said Josie, "aye, about then." Dan cut in.
"He said the same thing to me, Gary. He seemed very down." said Dan.
"Did you want to see him for something in particular?" asked Josie sipping her G&T.
"Not really, just keeping an eye on him."
"Well, I'd like to say he's over the worst but.." Josie's voice tailed off ominously. Where the hell had she really been, Loney wondered, and where was Jojohn? But Dan intervened again.
"I've been thinking about that McChesney business, Gary, and it's occurred to me that Josie here might be able to give you a few hints about Leonard Wylie. You were going out with him at that time, weren't you, Josie," he asked, "just before he took up with Norma, I suppose?"
"Briefly, very briefly," she said tartly and glowered fleetingly at the older man.
"I thought it was longer," said Dan, puzzled.
"A car salesman? As if!" Josie downed the G&T in one gulp.
"Aye, right enough, for you had your own wee business then, I remember," said Dan mildly. Loney got in fast.
"This your scarf?" The moment he asked the question, Loney knew he had said the wrong thing but got the right answer.
"Nope! Now when you see my grandchild, let him know I want a word with him." Josie's hand slammed down the glass hard onto the table, shattering the glass to pieces.

"Aw," said the astonished Dan, "there was no need for that, Josie." They all looked at Josie's hand as spots of blood began to ooze out slowly from her finger-tips. She took a long, deep breath before slapping aside the inept barman's hand. His cloth remained pristine.

"Leave it!"

"But."

"Just go back behind the bar, son," advised Loney quietly, "I'll deal with it." Auld Dan beat it fast along with the boy. He could read the signs although he did not actually understand precisely what they meant. Loney faced Josie. "Where is Jojohn?"

"Asleep with his fathers as it would say in the Bible. I'm trying to keep this in words you might just understand, Reverend Loney. Or Jojohn would have been if I'd not forgotten to sign the back page of our agreement." She pointed to the large legal document in front of her, now liberately splattered with blood. Loney was suddenly aware of the silence now pervading the bar. Most customers had already quickly left. Josie suddenly shouted,

"Lizzie Loudon, lock that door and keep them all in here or Loney dies!" The knife came from nowhere and shattered Loney's left arm. Lizzie locked the door. Loney's hand automatically went to his arm as he tried to stem the flow of blood.

"Josie, let them go," he pleaded quietly with her. Josie Duguid ignored him. She laughed suddenly, a deep, disturbing sound, and Loney felt his heart rate quicken appreciably.

The Ginger Bottle

"Wylie thought her show-biz connections were exotic. Wonder what he'd think now I've got an audience just hanging on my every word?"

"Where is he, Josie, where's Leonard Wylie?"

"Where is he?" asked Josie, "where are they? You name the order, Mr Loney. Work backwards or work forwards?" Loney said nothing for Josie was only listening to her own performance. The knife which pointed straight at him, a few inches away, never wavered as she moved slowly to the chair beside him. A drop of his own blood dripped onto his coat. "He loved me, he loved me not." Josie looked into his deep blue eyes. "His eyes were the same colour as yours and he was also another lying bastard like you and your promises."

"What promises, Josie?"

"Yours! Oh, I don't know. So what? I'll pay off all my debts and build a small empire. I'll go back to Perth, maybe visit the happy couple on the way and tell them all about it. I do that sometimes, you know, visit them in their flowery graves. Don't move!" she screamed suddenly at the remaining customers, but they all did till at last only Josie, Lizzie, Loney and the hapless barman were left.

"Like another drink, Josie?" asked Lizzie loudly from behind the bar. It was, after all, her pub.

"No, thank you, and Loney doesn't want one either."

"Do you mind if I have one?" said Lizzie.

"Go ahead and remember that by the time you've thrown something at me or the police arrive, I'll be dead and so will the minister here." Lizzie nodded and poured the barman a stiff dram. "How did you figure it all out, Mr Smart-Alec?" asked Josie laughing loudly. But a short slip of the knife along the back of his hand told all there that she had her agenda and intended sticking to it. Josie Duguid was not really interested in Loney's calculations and he knew it.

"You were saying," he said as he watched his own blood run in red rivulets down onto his coat. He swore under his breath at the mess it was making of the only decent bit of clothing he possessed.

"So I was. He said he hadn't, I said he had. Marriage, a proposal. I saw it coming, nobody else did. They were off and I was pregnant. Didn't tell him, though. Don't worry, the baby wasn't Kenna. But I was right all along for Fate stepped in and proved it." At last Loney knew where all this was going.

"Your little van, your mobile hairdressing business came to your aid, didn't it, Josie." She nodded her head vehemently.

"It was my nemesis, 'Josie's Gems'. You'll never believe this but I only dropped into the bus station by chance to use the facilities." Josie howled with laughter but stopped just as suddenly. "I sold it just after and then set up the shop. 'Killer Kuts!' What a laugh. Jojohn thinks he thought up that name but it had been in my mind all along."

"Just after what, Josie?"

"After I'd killed the two of them. Listen, want a laugh? Well, I saw them at the bus station waiting for a bus to Perth. Being the kindly person I am – you've said that yourself, Reverend Loney – I gave them a lift, told them I was going home for a few days, had a quick little picnic in the woods on the way, and that was that. I still have the scissors to this day. In fact, they're in daily use in the salon." Loney hoped like fury Jojohn hadn't used them on him that morning.

"What about the postcards?" asked Loney wondering where the boys in blue were for surely someone had phoned them.

"My idea," said Josie proudly. "I persuaded Norma to write two to her family and I posted them two months later while on holiday in New York. Just the plain sort we used to use in the old days. Leonard Bloody Wylie had his severance pay in his wallet and Norma McChesney had her savings all neatly placed in a little leather coin purse, all nicely folded into a tiny wee square. I blew most of it on an Atlantic sailing to New York, spent the rest on absolutely nothing of any value. That let them see what I really thought of them. They were worthless trash, the pair of them." The bile was hard-written all over Josie's face.

"They loved each other, Josie," said Loney quietly. Josie laughed at the very idea.

"It was just the show-biz element with him, that's all. Norma just happened to get in the way." She looked straight at Loney and shrugged. That was all the girl's life had meant to Josie Duguid.

"And my da, Josie, what about him?"

"Debt solution, that's all." She was quieting down now and Loney wondered how he might get her to put down the knife.

The Ginger Bottle

"Has Jojohn killed himself, Josie?" Loney asked.

"Sure. I'm now officially debt-free and it's great," she said. "Another G&T, please Lizzie."

"There's a helluva lot of racket coming from Mr Loney's room, Lizzie," shouted the barmaid breezing into the bar from nowhere. Another fortuitous comfort stop, thought Loney, somewhere in his raging mind. Jojohn was not dead, he was upstairs in Loney's flat.

"No!" screamed Josie as she rushed for the stairs. But Loney beat her to it. She lunged at the barman, drew blood from his forearm and shot out of the back door and into the yard. The backstairs in the alley were her destination, her access to Loney's flat and her grandson.

"Josie, can I make an appointment for a cut and blow-dry next Tuesday? Oh my God, hen, have you hurt yourself? Here, just you sit up and we'll have a look." A sudden pressure on her shoulders made the woman stand back from Josie Duguid's lifeless body.

"This way, ma'am." The woman dragged her gaze away from the now-sightless eyes, perplexed and bewildered by what had just happened, and allowed herself to be led out of the cobbled alley behind The Ginger Bottle by a police constable.

"She tripped. I called out to her about a booking, she looked back at me and she tripped, just tripped back down the stairs. Only four of them, too. Just shows you, doesn't it?" Showed exactly what, she had no idea. "Why did she have that knife in her hand? Helping Lizzie out in the kitchen, I suppose, don't you? I expect I'll just have to cross the street to

Killer Kuts and make the booking myself. Tuesday's one of her two OAP discount days, you see."
"Not right now, dear, just have a seat in the police car first, get over the shock. Fancy a cup of tea?"
"Are you Shona McPheator's boy?" the woman asked as she got in. The fifty-two year old 'boy' nodded and smiled. He had a feeling that his mother might just be on the phone to him later that day.

The area was now swarming with police, both uniform and plain-clothes, and Lizzie's inept barman had already handed in his notice verbally as his hands could not stop shaking long enough to write. His employer had already agreed that he need not work his notice. Every cloud has a silver lining, Lizzie Loudon thought.

Chapter 9

Loney threw open the door to the flat and skidded to an abrupt halt.
"This is some bit of kit you've got here, Uncle Gary."
"The TV? Like it? Great sound, too. It's Lizzie's. The flat's fully furnished but I'm still trying to persuade her that she needs a new sofa. How did you get in? Heard you had gone for a walk?" Loney hoped he sounded normal for he certainly did not feel like it.
"That back door's easy to open without a key. Lizzie should have it fixed. Just nudged it a little, a bit of pressure and it flew open. The insurers won't like that."
"I'm just collecting some notes. See you." Loney trudged downstairs, relieved that Jojohn was fine and spoke to the detective inspector.
"Everything's alright with Jojohn," he said quietly." DI McGrory seemed satisfied.
"I've put a watch on the outside stairs to your flat, Mr Loney. That'll give you a bit of peace from the local thrill-seekers. I take it that the boy's up there?" Loney nodded.
"That's about it. I'll leave his mother to tell him what's been happening," he said leaning against the wall. He felt wiped out.
"I'll have a word or two with you to help clear all this mess up once you've seen a doctor," DI Alec McGrory suggested, pointing to Loney's arm. They both watched the blood continue to pour down his arm and onto the floor. "Lizzie won't like it," said

McGrory smiling as the pool of blood widened on the floor.
"A bit of bleach will do the trick on the floor and a few stitches on the arm and hand. A word whenever you like, mate, for I'm not going anywhere except the cemetery. Got a few respects to pay. The boy knows very little."

Loney sat with Auld Dan and Kenna on the flat, table-stone memorial in Old Calton Burial Ground. He looked closely at it for the first time and then burst out laughing. It had weathered quite badly but was still legible.
'In loving memory of Helen McChesney who departed this life on 6th February 1854. May she and her family rest in eternal peace.' He read it out to the others and for a moment or two, a deep silence reigned.
"I expect they will now, Gary," said Kenna, her mobile nowhere in sight.
"You should be with Jojohn at the police station," said Loney sharply and did not know why for Kenna had just lost her mother.
"I didn't suspect my ma for a minute," Kenna answered sadly – for her – and neither man there believed her. Folk came and went in her life. Nobody cared as far as she was concerned and she certainly did not either. Loney said nothing. "Did you?" she asked half-interested. Gary Loney shook his head.
"I knew nothing at the beginning, nothing at all."
"So, what happened?" Old Dan McNab had an insatiable curiosity.

"Do tell," said Kenna brightly then her shoulders dropped a few centimetres, her voice quavered a little. "It was all what Dan here said. Leonard Wylie had been deserted by his own parents, brought up by his grandparents. Norma was more or less in the same boat. Now, was that enough to draw them together, make all the other dates seem very shallow? Quite possibly. To me it seemed that far from being a simple elopement that could easily have blown itself out, it was a very serious and lasting love affair. They were two people who understood each other very deeply. As nothing except a postcard or two from Norma was ever heard from her, I began to wonder why. Why break off all relationships with people she loved and who had taken care of her so well for most of her young life? It didn't make any sense. Then suddenly I wondered about my own father. Had he really followed them that day? Had he really been totally consumed, consumed beyond all reason, enough to follow them? And if he had caught up with them, then what? Leonard had left with Norma that day in his company car. What had actually happened?" But Dan jumped in quickly.

"That car of your da's was clapped out. He'd have been better trying to follow them on his bike. That's what he used for his work, his bike." Dan stared accusingly at Loney as he sat on the flat memorial stone. "Jackie was a very honourable man," he insisted. "Those rumours going around hurt him considerably. I can assure you that he was not implicated in that business at all. I worked with him, right beside him, in the factory that day." Dan was beginning to lose his cool and Loney hurried to placate the old man.

"I know that, Dan, I know that," he said softly.

"Don't encourage him, Gary, he's just a daft old bugger," said Kenna viciously. Dan stood up fast.

"I'm off. You want to get a grip of yourself, hen, and keep a civil tongue in your thick head," he yelled, his voice reverberating round the deserted graveyard. Fat Face kept well out of it under the tree that had figured in Robert Loney's imagined suicide bid. Kenna shrugged.

"Sorry. Sit down and have a chocolate éclair." Kenna offered the bag of sweets all round.

"Are they Cadbury's?"

"Aye, Dan, they are," said Kenna and frowned deeply as the old man took three then sat back down. Dan was easily bribed. Gary continued, well-used to such happenings.

"That scuppered that idea as it seemed to be a universally held truth. The police who had been very reluctant to get involved, had come to the same conclusion. So, folks, what had happened next? It seems the car Leonard had been using had been given up as required the day when he had finished working his notice, the day of the elopement. Where did the couple go?

"America," Kenna suggested chewing thoughtfully on her éclair. Loney shook his head. "Well, it seems she'd talked of that often enough," argued Kenna.

"Talking about it and doing it are two entirely different things. Nope. I thought of trains or coaches. The coach would be cheaper. Supposing they didn't catch a coach because a very kind friend met them in the bus station and offered them a lift to Perth and suggested maybe a short honeymoon in the famous Salutation Hotel there. Unfortunately, that journey, instead of being a great beginning for their future, it was the beginning of their end. But that friend could have been anyone. The real question was who had a car – or a van? Lizzie's father's photo did the trick for, behind those guests at that wedding all those years ago - yes, Dan, it was a copy of Mr Loudon's photo my da had - there was, in the background, a small van. 'Josie's Gems'. Had Josie been a spurned lover? A few words with Dan here told me all I wanted to know. Then Josie confirmed the whole thing in The Ginger Bottle. It seems that when Josie saw the two of them in Buchannan Street Bus Station, opportunity presented itself and she grabbed it with both hands." Again, silence reigned until Dan spoke.

"Will their remains ever be found?" he asked sadly, unwrapping his third éclair. He looked closely at it and then put it into his mouth.

"Who knows," answered Loney, "that all depends on Josie. She was the one who'd encouraged Jojohn to keep a diary. Maybe she kept one herself." Both he and Dan thought that neither Josie nor Kenna, for that matter, could keep her mouth shut for any length of time. They hoped that carried over into the written word.

"Sounds reasonable," Kenna said, the mobile once more in her hand. "But why did she murder Jackie?" She looked at Loney and then slowly slipped her mobile back into her bag. Nobody did disapproving looks like the Reverend Gary Loney.

"Debt," sighed Loney, "his money. She knew it would eventually come to Jojohn if his da hadn't squandered it all first. She had no idea that Da would skip Robert in favour of Jojohn. It was your telling her that it was all left to Jojohn – not his grandson, you will recall – but just Jojohn for Da knew as well as everyone else that the boy wasn't related to him." Auld Dan was loving this in a reluctant sort of way. "But Da loved him as if he were." Kenna's face was like stone and Loney suddenly thought how like her mother she looked. "Her first victim this time was Da, just before she drove Jojohn to Perth. She now knew that Jojohn would inherit the flat and insurance money because of your information Kenna. She was heavily in debt because of all her renovations to the shop and panic completely replaced all decent thoughts in her mind. She would kill my da and then, having got Jojohn into a partnership in Perth, she would be high and dry once young Jojohn was dead. All his debts would be paid and she would once more be debt-free. A very heady thought. The whole thing simply revolved round the necessity to clear her debts and start again. It was all, really, just a solution to meltdown – too much renovation too soon. Josie was under a tremendous amount of pressure but under none when she killed the first two. She had decided to try to encourage Jojohn commit suicide, actually thought he had. He's in a very vulnerable position right now because of Rhys's death." Kenna thought for a while before speaking, Dan shook his head at it

The Ginger Bottle

all and Loney felt like death itself at all the misery one person had caused.

"What about Rhys," asked Dan, "what about what he shouted?"

"Tell Loney to watch out?" said Loney. Dan nodded. "All very simple. He wasn't speaking about Jojohn, he was speaking about me. He was looking after his pal, saying that I was to watch out for the boy. Jojohn was always Duguid, never Loney." Silence reigned for a while.

"What'll happen to Killer Kuts?" asked Kenna.

"I expect Jojohn will fall heir to that, too. It'll be in the written partnership agreement. The part Josie hadn't signed had nothing to do with the main agreement. It was an additional one to do with equipment, a quite innocuous part. He has a lot of ideas but is very canny with his money, Kenna. I doubt if he'll want any input from the Duguids," said Loney quite brutally.

Gary Loney watched as the other two left the graveyard. It was a lovely peaceful place despite being just off the extremely busy Abercromby Street and he found himself reluctant to leave.

"Any tips for tomorrow, Mr Loney?" Wee Mrs Singleton appeared by his side. "I like to give a wee hint or two to some of our homeless, for being homeless doesn't mean you're not allowed a wee punt. Something for the connoisseur, not the masses who read The Glasgow Morning News." She already had her notebook and pencil in her hand.

"I'm giving it all up, Mrs Singleton, leading the simple life from now on." Loney still did not rise,

The Ginger Bottle

Mrs Singleton still did not move on. "The Trumpet Sounds, tomorrow at Ayr, 2.30pm." Mrs Singleton scribbled furiously.

"Thanks, minister. Must go," she said, "for it's my turn for the flowers in the church. Sorry about your da. He had hired a car that day those two eloped, did you know that? Heard you talking to Dan about it." She smiled slightly at him. "Dan McNab talked a whole lot of garbage to the police about that day. Neither one of them was at work all that day. Their mates covered for them for they went to watch a European football match just along the road when they should have been on the back shift. The car meant they saw the first-half and got back in time to finish the shift. The guy on the gate was Dan's brother. What a pair they were, Dan and your da," she said laughing at the memory as she hurried away. Loney hoped The Trumpet Sounds would win for her.

Loney left the graveyard and walked briskly up Abercromby Street. He would now have a cocktail with Summer in the new wine-bar cum bistro. New life, new Loney!

"Here's your tea and a buttered tattie scone, Gary, and a pile of sympathy cards that were handed in today. Mind if I join you?"

"My pleasure entirely, Lizzie." Well, old habits died hard, didn't they? And Loney was definitely an 'old habits' man.

Mitchell Memoranda Series
The Ranks of Death (Book 1)

The Realms of Death (Book 2)

The Rites of Death (Book 3)

Dom Broadley Series (Young Adult)

Don't Go There! (Book 1)

Tell me the Secret (Book 2)

Gorbals Chronicles Series
Once Upon a Murder (Book 1)

Death is Murder (Book 2)

Pure dead Murder (Book 3)

Printed in Great Britain
by Amazon